ELLE HARTFORD

How to Care for Cursed Fish

Marine Magic #1

In nature nothing exists alone.
~Rachel Carson

Contents

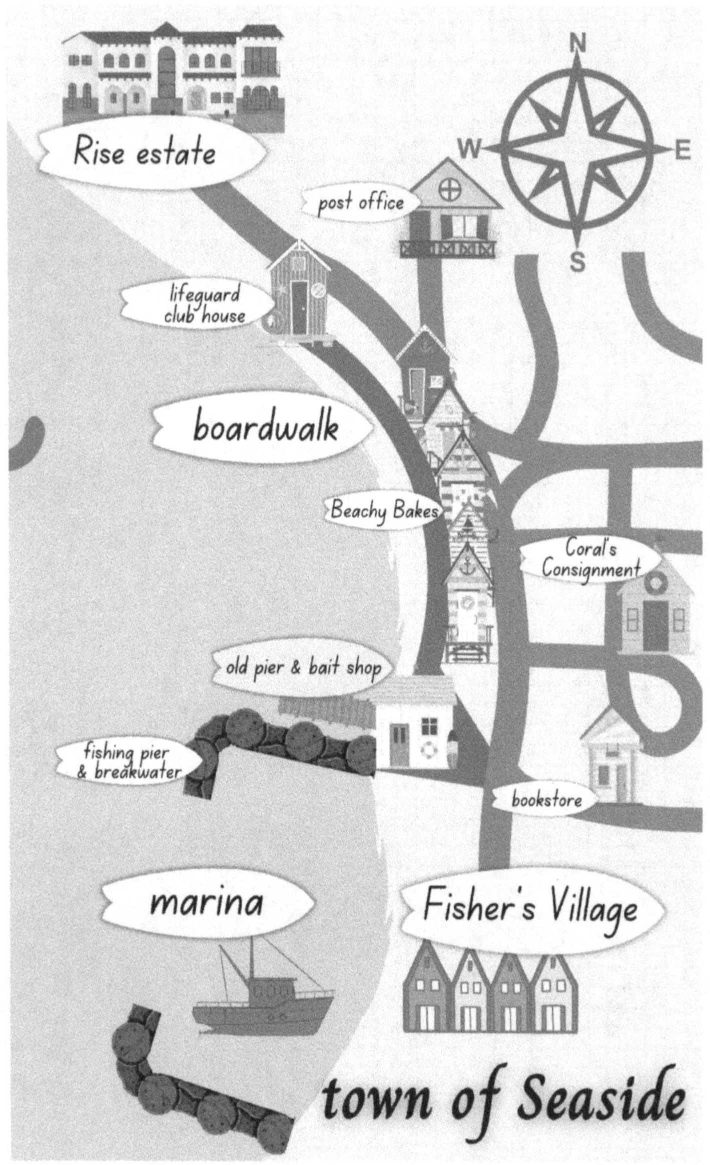

Rise estate
post office
N
W
E
S
lifeguard
club house
boardwalk
Beachy Bakes
Coral's
Consignment
old pier & bait shop
fishing pier
& breakwater
bookstore
marina
Fisher's Village
town of Seaside

Prologue

The most life-changing calls come when they're least expected.
Every student learns this lesson sooner or later . . .

"Haven? I need you to do something for me."

"Coming, professor!"

Theirs were the only two voices in New West Key University's
Marine Center and Animal Hospital, Quarantine Wing. It
was after hours. Gentle twilight fell in through the skylights,
casting white floors, walls, and holding tanks with an undersea
glow. Even the charmed sconces set into the walls had dimmed,
as they were programmed to do at the end of every work day.

But Sunlit Haven did not believe in work days. Though her
voice was deep and calm as twilight when she answered her
professor's call, her boots padded across the tile with haste. Her
veterinary scrubs, plain sandy cotton spelled to resist all but
the worst stains and spills, covered her up from neck to ankle.
Her hands were full, a clipboard, an extra pen, a roll of gauze, a
bottle of salt water purifier, a sadly scraped-up gooseneck clam
in the crook of her elbow. Her hair too was occupied, chopped
short and bound back under a white handkerchief. Pink hair,
light eyes, yellow skin—her grandmother had nicknamed
her "Sherbet," but Sunlit rarely had time for desserts, iced
or otherwise. She was the marine veterinary school's most
devoted student.

Even before she reached her professor at the observation

platform overlooking a pool of recuperating seals, Sunlit began talking again. "I have the gauze you were looking for, Professor. The viral wing has all been fed and locked down for the night, too. And I thought maybe you could check on Corduroy again. His shell's not cleaning up the way I'd hoped it would."

"Yes, yes," the professor murmured. She accepted the gauze and the update without comment, her attention caught between the seals and a bundle of mail in her hand. Considerably older than Sunlit, with long graying hair and a lab coat decorated with schools of cavorting dolphins, Professor Lina McAlpin looked nowhere near as intimidating as her reputation indicated. She was, in fact, a little distracted. After a pause, she leaned against the observation railing and looked at Sunlit, one eyebrow raised over dark green eyes. "You named the clam, Haven?"

"Not—really?" Sunlit's gaze shifted guiltily. "I know we're not supposed to. I didn't do it *consciously*. I just thought—it felt like—he told me, somehow."

The professor's gaze dropped to the clam in question. "Corduroy?"

Sunlit's answer was near a confessional whisper. "He's very proud of the ridges in his shell."

"All the more reason to get them cleaned up, then." Lina smiled, her eyes nearly lost in tanned wrinkles. "Another of your feelings, Haven?"

"Yes but he's very insistent about it," Sunlit said, holding the clam out to her mentor. "I mean—that is—it's really just another feeling, yes."

Professor McAlpin said nothing more as she looked over the clam. She'd been teaching Sunlit Haven for six years, from Intro to Marine Invertebrates all the way to supervised apprenticeships in the veterinary center, and she was familiar with Sunlit's *feelings.* They never came with any proof or corroboration. Sunlit herself seemed embarrassed by them. They weren't scientific, but she insisted they weren't magical, either. And yet, they often led to the right treatments and happy animals.

The clam's shell *did* need extra care. It had been subjected to a poisonous substance, one that could eat away at the little calcium carbonate creature if left unchecked. Professor McAlpin looked back up to see Sunlit crouched down against the walls of the glass holding tank, making faces at the seals. The seals nodded back and clapped their flippers in underwater laughter when Sunlit's collection of pens fell to the ground.

"I've got some of that extra-strength gentle cleansing potion left in my office," the professor said, as if she hadn't witnessed anything. "I'll take Corduroy there now and make a place for him overnight so I can check him in the morning. In the meantime, I want you to read over this letter. I'll be right back."

As she handed an opened envelope to Sunlit, she added, "See what feeling you get from it."

Sunlit straightened up and leaned against the tank walls, obediently focused on the letter as her professor walked away. The envelope was nothing extraordinary, aside from a water stain in the bottom left corner. It was addressed, rather sloppily, to "Whom it May Concern" at the University's Marine Research school. Curious, but only mildly so, Sunlit pulled out the letter, which had been folded just once. The torn piece of paper read,

To the New West Key U researchers. They say you're the best. Here at Seaside we've got something you'll want to see. A giant otter crashed into the old fishing pier in the storm overnight. It needs

attention and someone to talk to. Send reply ASAP or better yet send someone. Town vet won't have anything to do with magical creatures. We need someone with more expertise.

Sunlit read it twice, and still wasn't sure what she thought when her professor returned.

"Well?" Lina took the letter back and glanced at it herself, ignoring the seals who watched over Sunlit's shoulders. "I think it's worth checking out. But—"

"But, Professor," protested Sunlit, "you have the conference in two days."

Professor Lina smiled. "Yes, there is the conference, and plenty left to do. So—I'll have to send someone, don't you think?"

"It does seem like a good idea," Sunlit agreed. "The poor otter probably needs attention right away. Of course, they don't specify, but an old dock probably means splinters and bruises and—"

The professor held up a hand, and Sunlit went quiet, blushing. Behind her, the seals bobbed above the water's surface and raised their flippers, thinking this was a "follow-the-leader" game.

"So," repeated Lina. "Who do you think I should send?"

Sunlit hesitated. The marine veterinary program was small and elite, the only one of its kind in all Beyond. All its graduates were capable. However, some focused primarily on research; some had family or other reasons they needed to stay in New West Key; and others couldn't quite be trusted to properly clean a clam without assistance . . .

"The letter's from Seaside," Lina observed. "That's quite a distance. They'll need someone who doesn't have to immediately come back here, for schoolwork or other reasons.

And they'll need someone who's good at thinking on her feet. Someone who has completed extensive study, who isn't afraid of travel, and above all, someone who *listens* to animals."

By that point, Sunlit had caught the professor's drift. Her pale yellow cheeks flushed again. "You don't really mean *me*? But there's so much I have to do here!"

"Sunlit Haven," said the professor, severely, "you have been doing work here for years. You have *graduated* and you are still doing work here. You completed your apprenticeship in only a year, and still, here you are."

"The other students need help," Sunlit protested. "And the Center always needs more hands. I run study sessions . . ."

"You do good work," Lina agreed, her tone purposeful. "And that is why you are the one I want to send, Haven."

"But . . ." Sunlit shook her head. Behind her, the seals shook too, sending water droplets over the tank wall and across her shoulders. She didn't notice. She was looking for excuses, but found she'd run out. With her grandparents passed away and her aunt on leave, she really didn't have much reason to stay in New West Key. It had simply become—comfortable.

Professor Lina had seen many students come and go. Her voice was kindly. "Will you do this, Haven? I think it might be the opportunity that you need."

Sunlit gulped. She wasn't so sure about that. But she *did* know there was an otter out there that needed help, stat. So she straightened her shoulders and nodded her head.

"I'll do it," she agreed. "And who knows—I might even be back in time for the conference."

1

An Accidental Joy

The giant otter is known primarily for its occasional appearance in old texts, in which aquatic mercenaries were described as riding ox-sized otters as mounts. The breed is exceedingly rare today. It is thought that there may be a colony of giant otters residing in the northwest waters, but as yet no scientist has located them. In general, the giant otter is a strong and clever animal, capable of speech and reason. It has no magic of its own, but retains the sharp senses and the athletic personality that makes its smaller, average counterparts so beloved .

. .

—From Traverse's Guide to Marine Vertebrates, Invertebrates, and Magical Outliers

Seaside was not a town that could be quickly left.

A giant otter had discovered this the night before, and Sunlit would find it out in her own time. The town curved along the ocean waves, crescent-shaped like the moon, but full of sunny faces and bright attractions. A colorful boardwalk lined with enterprising food and game stalls paralleled the beach. Behind it, Main Street featured everything from potions shops and bookstores to hermit crab adoption centers and sailboat rentals. At the north end of town, the land rose into a majestic bluff, atop which sat grand estates for the elite. At the southern end of town, the beach gave way to a working harbor. A long fishing pier marked the point between the two.

Indeed, the pier had often been a point of contention between those in the town who liked fishing, and those in town who liked tourists. Some decades back, the official pier had been rebuilt and moved just slightly to the south, a compromise in which the fishers got nice new fish-cleaning sinks and anti-odor spells, while the beach goers got slightly more room. However, nothing had ever become of the old pier, sandwiched between fish markets and family outings. Its farthest reaches had eroded into the sea, but a good twenty yards of old wood plank remained, hovering a few feet above high tide. Where the pier connected to the boardwalk there was a plaza, the sort of place that might have made an idyllic little town garden or event space, if it weren't for the unsightly old bait shop. The property had long been abandoned and belonged to the town, but the town could never quite agree on what they wanted to do with it.

They'd never considered the possibility that an otter as big as a young dragon and heavy as a blacksmithing giant's anvil might crash into it.

The winds that night had been fierce, pushing the waves high and southward. In the darkness and confusion, much of the shoreline had been damaged. Storms were a fact of life along the ocean, particularly in early spring. But no one in Seaside had ever seen anything like this.

Sunlit hadn't, either. Still woozy from making use of the postal service's handy—if temperamental and still rather new—teleportation system, and leaning to one side under the weight of her hastily-packed knapsack, Sunlit was not in the best state of mind to process the sight.

After a quick telegram to Seaside's town council and a trip home to collect her things, Sunlit had traveled to the little town as quickly as she could. She managed to arrive later the same evening, mere hours after reading a strange letter in the quiet of the Marine Center. While the postal service all across Beyond tended to rely on magitech, things like telegram wires and old-fashioned letters, more and more post offices offered a magical teleportation service, too. Though they mostly used it to send on urgent letters, some enterprising souls made it their transport mode of choice. It was expensive and unpleasant and a little bit risky, but just the thing when a giant otter's life was at risk.

Sunlit might have been hesitant to take on the responsibility, but once it was hers, she certainly wouldn't let a hurt otter down. Her home in New West Key was shared with her aunt, after all, and not truly hers; it was easy to collect her reference books and a few traveling things before rushing out. One such traveling thing was her ancient blue parrot, Biscuit. The bird clung to her hand, spouting obscenities perhaps related to its recent mode of travel.

It was in this state that Sunlit met Officer Ebb, the police chief in Seaside.

"Town council received your telegram and asked me to take

you straight to the pier," he informed Sunlit, over the raucous protests of the parrot. He had the tan skin, pointed ears, and blue eyes of many coastal elves. His hair was graying, tucked beneath a brimmed hat. His smooth, if aged, face gave away no irritation nor amusement. "Unless you want to stop by a hotel first?"

"No." Sunlit was definite about that, at least. She'd been able to expense the teleportation cost to the university, and they'd likely pick up her hotel costs too, but she hadn't yet planned that far ahead. "Let's get to the pier. Can you tell me exactly what happened? Is the otter very badly injured?"

"You'd know best about that," Officer Ebb said, as they fell into step. They left the low-slung post office building side by side and started down a sandy road into town. "Of course, it might tell you, itself. I've had my hands full just keeping civilians away from the remains of the pier."

Sunlit tugged a wide-brimmed hat down over her bandanna-covered hair, hiding her face from the evening sun. "If that's the case, then who wrote to the university?"

"From what I hear, Chip assigned himself that task." Officer Ebb, who stood a foot taller than Sunlit and cut a dashing figure in his blue uniform, sounded a bit helpless in the face of this development. "He was the one who officially discovered the wreckage, you might say."

"Does he work at the pier?" Sunlit asked, her mind mostly on otters.

"No one does. Chip's one of the fishers. The old pier was about to be condemned, if I'd had my say. I'm still trying to convince the council to either take it down or sell it. Of course, that's no easy task with an otter in the way."

This got Sunlit's attention. "What do you mean? Can't the

otter be moved?"

"I gather that's what they called you in to decide," Officer Ebb said dryly. He steered them down a little alley off of Main Street, adding, "You'll see for yourself in a minute."

As they emerged onto the boardwalk, Sunlit tugged again at her hat and loose sleeves, avoiding the glare of the last rays of sun off the water. It took her a minute to make sense of the scene. The beach stretched to their right, dotted with people carrying trash bags and sticks—a clean up effort. To the left, the solid wall of merchants' stalls divided them from Main Street, and many of the merchants themselves were tidying their wares or re-enforcing spell-protected windows. The old pier was down at the other end of the beach. Sunlit could see how debris had been washed up onto the pier and caught against the breakwater, a massive structure of boulders that supported the new fishing pier beyond. She could see, too, how one of the light posts had fallen along with the wreckage, effectively barring anyone from going out onto the little pier. Slightly further out, an old boat had been driven against the breakwater and held in place by a mess of buoys and nets. In the shadow of that mess, Sunlit could just barely see dark fur.

The more she saw, the quicker she walked. With his long legs, Officer Ebb kept pace with her. The planks of the boardwalk disappeared under her increasingly anxious strides. By the time they'd neared the old pier, Sunlit was running. The parrot, having given up on being carried gracefully, flew overhead.

"Chief!" A young officer standing sentry at the edge of the old pier hailed Officer Ebb. A woven purple lanyard bore her name tag, which read *Sabrina, she/her* in careful serif font above the town seal. Sunlit registered this without a second thought; New West Key University was large and efficient, and employed a similar form of identification for students and professors. Sabrina, a rounded, diminutive figure with a long black ponytail and violet eyes that matched her lanyard, shouted again. "Just a moment!"

Sunlit stopped on the tips of her toes, frustrated by the distraction. The downed light post blocked her way and meant that the pier was cast in shadow; she couldn't quite make out the mess behind it, where the otter lay.

"Any news?" Ebb asked the junior officer. The two of them stood beside an old building while Sunlit stared out along the pier, still searching for signs of her patient.

"The clean up crew wanted to get over here and start on the debris, but the council wouldn't let them," Sabrina informed them conscientiously, her painted nails flashing silver against her tan skin. She waved her hands frequently as she spoke. "Liability, and all that. Said the whole pier might still come down."

"So no one's been out to the otter?" Sunlit turned, outraged.

"Hello," called a faint voice from underneath the trapped boat. At twenty paces away, it was weak and watery.

"Hello!" Sunlit called back, instantly forgetting both officers. "How are you? Where are you hurt?"

"My tail," the voice mourned. "And a little bump on the head. And I just can't tell you how I'm dying for something to eat."

"Have you lost any blood?" Sunlit asked. She was very tempted to climb over the light post, but her boots were heavy, and her pack still held her back.

"Dear me, I don't know," came the reply. Now that the otter had found someone to talk to—as suggested in the letter, coincidentally enough—it seemed to be perking up. "But it's awfully cramped in here. I can't turn around, or I'd tell you for sure. What else would you like to know? Mind you, I don't remember anything after that anchor conked me in the head. I'm sure I do wish I could be of more use. You can call me Joy, did I ask for your name yet? Rude of me. I don't suppose any of those fish-fry stalls I smell deliver food?"

"We'll figure something out," Sunlit promised the otter. She turned once more, recollecting the officers. "I need to get out there, and I need food and clean water as soon as possible. I have a light and my medical kit, but I may need more once I get out there and take stock of the situation."

The junior officer glanced sideways up at Officer Ebb. "Is she allowed to go out there, sir?"

"Why wouldn't I be? Why else would you call me?" Sunlit's outraged words were echoed by Biscuit, who had perched on the pier above.

"Like I said, that was an *independent* call," Officer Ebb said, a trace of sourness touching the words. "Let's get the council out here. They should be done with the beach clean up by now."

"But we can't wait. It's already been so long," Sunlit cried. Her healer's mind was racing. An entire day in such chaotic conditions—any open wound stood a good chance of infection, and the otter had mentioned her head hurt as well . . .

Officer Ebb shrugged, his face registering none of the concern Sunlit felt. "The town owns the pier, and they have to look out for *everyone's* safety, not just the otter's."

"But surely," Sunlit protested, "the otter is *part* of 'every-one,' and if I'm offering to go out there of my own free will, then isn't that a good thing?"

"We have to observe procedure." The words sounded extensively practiced.

"I'll sign anything you want," said Sunlit. "I could go out

there to see, and then come back to sign things, if you don't have the paperwork now. But I really have to—"

"The town owns the pier. They have the final word," Officer Ebb repeated. Beside him, Sabrina reached for her belt with one glittering hand, as if instinctively readying a pair of handcuffs.

"What if *I* owned the pier?" Sunlit didn't know where the words came from. All she felt was the energy in her chest—the energy of a promise made to an animal in need. "I'll buy it. Right now. I'll take responsibility for it."

The young sentry dropped her handcuffs to the boards below with a metallic clatter.

Officer Ebb cleared his throat. "Either way, we'll need to have a talk."

2

A Dear Misunderstanding

> *First, as a matter of principle, an animal hospital must be set in the proper location. It must get plenty of natural light, have good drainage, and sturdy foundations. It is recommended that an animal hospital building be built specifically for its purpose. Repurposing an old building is not considered best practice . . .*
> —From Standard Practices for a Safe & Sanitary Animal Medic

It was a hasty proposal, but Sunlit wouldn't allow herself to go so far as *regretting* it. She did, however, feel a few minor qualms about the purchase.

Willing as the university might be to pay for teleportation or a few nights at a hotel, Sunlit knew they'd balk at buying seafront property. Not to mention that even if it *might* work out for the best in the long run, she didn't actually have the authority to make the purchase for the Marine Center. But she did have her inheritance from her grandmother—money that was totally her own, that she'd been hoarding carefully, never knowing what to spend it on . . .

And now, quite abruptly, there was a surprisingly fresh-faced and eager council member with them on the pier.

Officer Ebb made the introductions. It turned out the town council's representative was a mer-person named Taiwo Rise. Though her own thoughts were in turmoil, Sunlit registered the fact that Taiwo used the pronoun *they*, and acted with total confidence. Taiwo was tall, dark-skinned, with long black beaded hair and bright purple eyes—and an energy level that had not been affected by a day of picking up detritus on the beach.

"You're from New West Key? I heard we'd contacted the university," Taiwo said, enthusiastically shaking Sunlit's reluctant hand. "What can you do for the otter?"

"They won't let me do anything," Sunlit stammered, looking over at the police officers.

"Oh—yes—liability and all that. But I thought you'd think of a way around it," said Taiwo. "The University has suggested procedures, or something?"

"Miss Haven's suggested purchasing the pier," Officer Ebb said, in the dry tones which apparently came customary to him.

Taiwo's round face gleamed. "The university wants to buy the pier? That's perfect! You can put up an outpost of the Marine Center here—everyone in Seaside'd be thrilled. Everyone who knows what's good for them and the ocean, anyway."

"Well—" Sunlit stammered, both frightened by and rather taken by Taiwo's enthusiasm. "Not exactly—"

But Taiwo talked on. "And if they're worried about having to build a new pier, tell them it's no trouble. The main thing is just reinforcing the underwater supports. I can get help from the local mercamp for that if you're interested—they'd be so glad to help with a marine animals sanctuary, I can promise you that."

"Taiwo's mother is the leader of the local merfolk community," Officer Ebb told Sunlit in an undertone.

"And my partner's a business leader in town," Taiwo said brightly, "but never mind that. It's as council representative that I'm here, and I say, this is the best thing to happen in town for years. You wouldn't even *really* need to tear down the old bait shop. Unless you want to, of course—"

"Most people would want to," Officer Ebb said, continuing his asides.

"Never mind him. He's been grumpy about the old pier for decades," Taiwo told Sunlit. "Let's get a preliminary agreement out of the way right now so that you can get to work on freeing that otter. What do you think?"

"Well," Sunlit managed once more, "I have to tell you, I can't promise a new marine center. The university—I mean, they *did* send me—but I can't speak for them, not *that* much."

"But you *can* purchase the pier?" Taiwo's gaze on Sunlit was both hopeful and keen.

"I do have money," Sunlit admitted. "But it's—my own money."

"They can reimburse you afterward," Taiwo declared. "Or who knows? You can keep it yourself and run your own sanctuary. Do you like Seaside so far?"

"I really hadn't planned on staying," Sunlit admitted. She'd been in town all of half an hour. And there was a conference back in New West Key calling her name. "But—if this is how it works out best—"

"We can definitely figure out the details as we go along," said Taiwo. They were already waving over Sabrina and writing out the preliminary contract terms in the junior officer's notebook.

"I—I guess we can," Sunlit said. It was a revelation.

"And I'm going to make sure we give you a *really* good deal," Taiwo added. "After all, you're really doing us all a favor."

Taiwo tilted the notebook to show Sunlit a brief statement of their agreement and a sum that made her stomach flip. The figure was large . . . but not as large as her savings. And Joy the otter was still out there, waiting.

Sunlit looked up overhead, at the darkening sky, and at Biscuit. The parrot cried out over the pier, "*We can! We can!*"

"Right," said Sunlit. "I'll need to stay as long as it takes the otter to recuperate, anyway." Maybe, she thought, it would be cheaper to buy a pier than to stay in one of the town's fancy hotels . . . provided the bait shop really was habitable.

"Welcome to town," Officer Ebb told her ruefully.

"You're going to love it here," added Taiwo, holding the notebook steady for Sunlit to sign.

* * *

Another half hour later, Sunlit was ten yards down her pier, tugging at fallen beams and avoiding rusty nails under Biscuit's watchful eye. Taiwo had gone off to report to the rest of the council with a spring in their step. The junior officer remained on standby, now not so much a guard as a bemused bystander, and Officer Ebb had—with a heavy sigh—gone back to the police station to make a report of his own.

Sunlit was glad for the quiet, and for something to do. The sun was setting, but she didn't mind; in fact, she felt more free in the dark. Despite her name and pale, bright coloring—or perhaps because of that latter fact—Sunlit avoided direct sunlight as much as possible. An inexplicable quirk of genetics had left her with *very* easily burned skin. A walk to the post box as a child had left her with blisters and raw patches for a week. Now, she adopted loose long sleeves, light gloves, and wide-brimmed hats as a matter of course.

She might have wished for heavier gloves in this circumstance, however. As much as thin gloves were helpful for examining marine animals by touch, they were not much protection from the rough, upended rubbish on the pier.

But that was not nearly enough to deter Sunlit. Particularly not with a giant otter talking her through the entire process.

"Normally I have very good hearing," the otter, Joy, assured Sunlit. "But it *is* difficult to hear anything through this boat. Maybe because it's so waterlogged. I can't complain, though, as that's made it nice and comfy today. Good thing it wasn't too warm a day, right? I suppose it is still *early* spring. But I confess I do like those winter months. And I haven't fully gotten in my summer coat yet. Did you say your name was Miss Haven?"

"Sunlit Haven. Either Sunlit or Haven is fine." Sunlit paused to wipe her brow, panting. In her mind, she cataloged what she had left to face: five yards of debris and uncertain planks, freeing the boat itself, tending to Joy's tail . . . and dealing with shedding otter fur, too, no doubt. Good thing she'd brought her pack with her: there were medical masks in there, just in case. Sunlit hadn't run across any animal she was allergic to, but it never hurt to be prepared.

"Very nice to meet you, Miss Haven. But what was I saying?"

said Joy. "Oh, yes. I couldn't quite hear what you were all saying down there. You aren't going to demolish the pier, are you? I would feel awfully bad."

"I would think you'll feel a whole lot better away from the pier," Sunlit pointed out, huffing as she slid another board into the watery depths below.

"Between you and me, I've rather come to like it. It's awfully fun to hear the kids on the beach nearby, don't you think?"

"I only just got here," Sunlit said, testing out the next plank to see if it would hold her weight.

"It's a very popular place for vacations," Joy told her, proudly, as though she'd had a hand in building up the town.

This got Sunlit to pause for a moment. "Are you from here, Joy?" If she wasn't, mending and *relocating* a giant otter might be an even bigger undertaking than anyone had expected.

"Oh, I'm not from anywhere in particular," Joy answered, a little hastily. "But I'd just arrived when the storm hit last night. I think I'll stay a while."

"That's a good attitude," Sunlit said. Especially since she couldn't, in good conscience, tell an otter with an injured tail to consider swimming at length any time soon. She jumped over a rotted plank and found herself facing the overturned boat, at last. Joy spoke, but for a moment, she wasn't paying attention. She was forced to ask, "I'm sorry, what was that, Joy?"

"I said, how long are you planning to stay?" the otter replied, as if they were fellow tourists meeting over tea.

"As long as it takes," Sunlit answered. She tried not to let the uncertainty creep into her voice. A heavy anchor chain was stretched across the hull of the rowboat, and with it, a hopelessly entangled mess of nets and weights. Somehow, all of the heaviest and most dangerous nautical doodads in the harbor seemed to have converged upon this point.

"You should consider staying longer," said Joy. "When did you last take a vacation?"

Sunlit answered off-hand as she cautiously circled the boat, looking for any complications that might hurt Joy when the boat was turned upright. Not to mention any suggestion of a place to start untangling the nets. "Well, they give us breaks between semesters at the university."

"How nice! And where did you go on your last break?"

"I didn't go anywhere," Sunlit answered, tugging at the anchor chain where it was exposed on one side. She'd already forgotten what they were talking about.

"A staycation, isn't that what they call it? I guess that's what I did today," said Joy, chuckling at herself.

"No, I worked at the Center," Sunlit said. With one more violent tug, she got the chain to slide down. It clanked against the pier and for a terrible moment, Sunlit thought they all might crash into the waters below. But the pier held, and now there was only netting to worry about.

"What do you do at the Center?" Joy asked innocently.

"I'm an assistant. I recently—graduated—" Sunlit huffed as she pulled nets apart with all her might—"the marine veterinary program. I never—thought about—what to do next."

"Why not?" asked Joy.

"My grandparents—needed someone—to help." Sunlit ripped one of the nets free, invigorated, not paying attention to personal details she usually chose not to reveal. It was her habit to talk to injured animals: it helped distract and calm them. That this one could talk back had already become commonplace. "And after my grandmother passed away, then I was staying with my aunt."

"Does she need help too?" Joy sounded genuinely curious.

"Not really," Sunlit admitted, as she shifted another net up over the prow of the boat. The truth was, she felt awkward in her aunt's home, a perpetual guest, despite her aunt's kindly nature. "Do you have any family, Joy?"

"None anymore," said the otter, with a trace of sadness. But with fortitude, she added, "Aside from the lovely new people I meet, of course. I think it's wonderful how people go out and find friends these days. Don't you, Miss Haven?"

"Mmm," Sunlit answered, more focused on the final net. By cutting it free from its weights with her multi-tool, she was able to dislodge it. "Joy, I think we're ready to move the boat. Can you let me know if it starts to get too close to any part of you?"

"I can do more than that," said Joy. "I can help you lift. My front paws are just fine. Shall we?"

"Wait—okay—okay," Sunlit puffed, as her frantic worry faded into relief. The boat went up easily, tipped, and fell toward the ocean side. Sunlit just barely managed to step out of the way.

"Oh dear, did you get hurt? I didn't even think," said Joy, twisting around.

Sunlit paused for a moment, hands on her hips, regaining her breath. In the twilight, she could see Joy for the first time. The otter was roughly the size of a horse, shorter perhaps on her stubby legs but much longer, her tail wrapped around her body before it twisted back at an uncomfortable angle. Her fur was deep brown and plush, a sign of a healthy diet to Sunlit's trained eye. Although she suspected that underneath all that fur, Joy might be a little underweight. The otter's face, however, was open and friendly, long whiskers underscoring warm, dark eyes and a large, expressive nose. Sunlit didn't see any obvious signs of damage that Joy hadn't mentioned already—but she did notice matted fur over the otter's face and blood staining the planks beneath her tail.

"I'm fine." Sunlit brushed off the question and immediately focused on her work. "I don't want to move you yet. Are you okay sitting where you are? You can make yourself more comfortable. I'm going to pull a light and some cleaning cloths out of my pack. You don't think there's any reason to worry about the pier supporting you, do you?"

"It held me and the boat and that anchor all day," Joy said reasonably, shifting to sit on her hip. "Where'd that anchor go, anyway? Oh, there it is. If only I had been able to reach it! We wouldn't have had all this bother."

"Nothing's a bother if it's helping you heal," Sunlit said automatically, as she extended the stand on her portable lantern.

"That's kind of you," said Joy. "I think this portion of the pier is perfectly fine, in any case. I don't see why they would want to take it down. You could have a party out here!"

Sunlit unfolded a sanitary, charmed white cloth and began sliding it under Joy's tail. Though she said nothing, caught up in her work, she was privately glad that there *wasn't* anyone else on the pier with them. Joy might be the sort who liked company, but Sunlit was hoping to focus and be done as soon as possible. Seaside had already been disorienting enough.

When a new voice joined them from below, Sunlit nearly toppled back into her lantern.

"Did someone ask for a party?"

3

A Meddlesome Friend

If surgery must occur in the open air, as is often the case with emergencies or very large animals, the proper help is essential. An assistant can ensure that tools remain clean and the space remains undisturbed. For open air surgeries, plan on twice the assistants of a routine surgery in-house.

—*from* Standard Practices for a Safe & Sanitary Animal Medic

Chip Daleson was not the sort to second-guess his own decisions. The most successful fishers develop an intuition, a sense for the sea, and Chip applied that feeling of *knowing* to his entire life. His family on both sides, going back for generations, had fished Seaside's waters. The fact that they were considered land-kin never gave a one of them pause.

To be -*kin* in Beyond was a magical thing. Most often it

was the result of literal magic, be it a curse, a pact, a wish, or a love affair with a magical creature. When an ancestor formed a transformative bond with some other creature, their descendants took on some of that creature's characteristics. One could be catkin, for example, with luminescent slitted eyes or claws; one might even be dragonkin, perhaps covered in beautiful patterns of scales; or one might be sharkkin, with tough skin and gills—as it was rumored a witchy hermit outside Seaside's borders might be. The impossible has yet to be discovered in Beyond.

Chip and his family were wolfkin. Chip himself appeared mostly human, stocky, male, pale-skinned—though not so prone to burning as Sunlit. But Chip also sported thick, cropped white hair, dark eyes, white wolfish ears, and a short white tail. *Fluffy* was the only word for it. Because it helped him keep his balance while clambering about a small fishing boat, Chip didn't mind it one bit.

The one thing Chip *did* mind was being taken for a werewolf. But that's straying somewhat from the point.

As Officer Ebb had noted, Chip had been the first one to notice the pier's collapse—and the otter in peril. Chip had also been the one to write to New West Key. Not all the town council members would have taken this with the benign enthusiasm Taiwo did. Fortunately, the thought of censure had never entered Chip's mind.

However he *did* know, perfectly well, that boating near the old pier was strictly forbidden by the communal beach rules. Not only was the pier itself dangerous, but the breakwater immediately south of it was even worse. An unfortunate boater caught between the pier and a rogue wave might not end up as lucky as Joy had.

And that's why Chip had waited until nightfall to return to the scene of his crime.

Sunlit sat heavily on her back pockets and stared down at the strange white face illuminated by her lantern. He was grinning up at her and Joy from a hole in the planks.

"It might not be party-worthy, but I brought food," he continued, holding up a paper bag. "Saw you working over here and figured you might want some."

"I smell fish!" declared Joy, who definitely wanted some.

Sunlit, on the other hand, was preoccupied by other matters. "Who are you? Are you allowed to be here?"

Chip tucked the bag under one arm and deftly tied his boat to one of the remaining supporting columns beneath the pier. He then scrambled up the pillar, using his own rope as a foothold, and swung himself onto the pier, barely missing a remaining section of railing.

"Hi," he said, sticking his hand out to Sunlit. "My name's Chip. I guess you could say I'm not supposed to be here. But I feel kind of responsible for you, since it was my letter and all. You *are* from the university, aren't you?"

"How could you tell?" Acting on autopilot, Sunlit shook his hand and then took the bag he offered, extracting a wrapped sandwich in order to inspect a container of wet fish. Apparently, Chip had brought separate meals for separate preferences.

Sunlit was nothing if not careful with the care of animals, however. Joy wriggled impatiently around her as Sunlit inspected each fish, noting its type and any signs of defect.

Meanwhile, Chip kept up a cheerful monologue. "I know *everyone* in town, but I don't know you. Is that your parrot up there, too? That's cool. I always wanted one, but Pa can't stand them. Sensitive ears. So are you, like, scoping things out for the university? I figured they'd have to send a whole team or something. Are you a professor there? Bet you've never seen a giant otter. My cousins thought I was lying about finding one trapped on the pier. What is it? Did you think I'd poisoned the fish or something?"

Sunlit passed the container over her shoulder to Joy, who took it daintily in her forepaws. As the otter slurped down fish one by one, Sunlit turned to Chip, who was watching her anxiously. She sighed. "No, I didn't think you'd poisoned them. Exactly. It's just that anyone who hasn't eaten for a day or more under stressful conditions has to be careful about what they *start* eating. You don't want anything too heavy, especially if some kind of surgery is needed."

"Whoa." Chip's deep brown eyes went wide. "Are you going to do a surgery? Here?"

"I was just trying to figure that out," said Sunlit, looking down at Joy's tail between them. "I don't think we'll need to, but this is serious. It needs to be stitched up and wrapped."

"I'd hate it if anything happened to *my* tail," Chip said sympathetically. "So, you must be some kind of expert if you know all that, right? I bet you've done this thousands of times."

"Um, I'm . . ." Sunlit bit her lip. Her impulse was to say *I'm just a student.* Still. Truthfully, she'd graduated over a year ago—as her professor had recently reminded her. And exactly how old did Chip think she was? He seemed like he was only a few years younger than her; he had the same enthusiasm she saw in undergraduates. But then, they also always thought she was old enough to be an experienced professor. An 'old soul,' that's what her grandmother had called her. "I'm not really an expert. Like you said, Joy is definitely the first giant otter I've ever seen."

"Oh, your name is Joy?" Chip looked up at the otter, his tufted ears perked. "Wow, sorry I didn't introduce myself earlier. Guess I got excited. I came by this afternoon, too, but I think you were asleep or something."

"Or unconscious," Sunlit worried, realizing that maybe Joy's "little bump on the head" was also something she needed to look into.

"Or something," Joy agreed, swallowing another fish whole. "These fish are very fresh. I forgive you for not introducing yourself. Just between us, I might have been a little hangry."

"I probably would be too," Chip said, scratching his head. "Hey, speaking of, why don't you eat your sandwich, Professor?"

Sunlit was hesitating, caught between saying *I really should clean up Joy first* and *I'm not actually a professor*, when a whistle pierced the night.

"DALESON!" A voice bellowed from the beach. "YOU KNOW THE RULES!"

"Oops," Chip said lightly to Sunlit and Joy. He hopped to his feet and stood against the old railing, leaning like it hadn't just barely-survived a massive storm, and shouted back with all his might. "THE RULES OF HOSPITALITY, YOU MEAN?"

Sunlit cowered from the noise, sheltering against Joy's side. Joy seemed preoccupied with the last of her fish.

"NO BOATS BY THE OLD PIER!"

"NO HEARTS ON THE BEACH!" Chip hurled back. He turned and glanced down at Sunlit, beaming. "Don't worry about him. That's just Ige. You'll probably meet him—"

"DON'T MAKE ME SWIM OUT THERE AND FINE YOU!"

"Actually, I'm surprised he hasn't yet," Chip commented to Sunlit. "These lifeguards, you know. But maybe he's tired from the clean up. JUST ADD IT TO MY TAB!" He added, turning back to face the darkened beach.

"*Add it to my tab! Add it to my tab!*" Biscuit agreed from the breakwater behind them.

"YOU HAVE TWO SECONDS BEFORE I COME OUT THERE!" warned the mysterious lifeguard Ige. Sunlit fervently hoped he hadn't heard Biscuit. She had no desire to get mixed up in this.

"HA! YOU DON'T HAVE THE GUTS!" Chip howled.

"AT LEAST MERFOLK HAVE SENSE," Ige roared. "AND *WE'RE* THE ONES WHO CAN BREATHE WATER!"

"I hate it when he pulls that on me," Chip told Sunlit. "Well, I guess I better be going. Where are you staying? The old bait shop? That way you don't have to move Joy, right? I've always wondered what it's like in there."

"ONE SECOND, DALESON!"

"I'D LIKE TO SEE YOU CATCH ME! Okay, see you later," Chip added, grinning at Sunlit one last time as he swung down into his boat through the hole in the pier. Before Sunlit could take a breath, Chip had freed the boat and was skipping away over the waves, powered by a small magitech motor.

In his absence the pier was eerily quiet. Sunlit waited for a moment, paralyzed, to see if Ige was about to show up to arrest Biscuit. Or herself.

"Well," said Joy, after one long moment alone had stretched into two, "this certainly does seem to be an *interesting* town."

* * *

Sunlit did, eventually, finish her examinations that night.

First was Joy, of course. Using cleansing and anesthetic potions from her medical kit, Sunlit managed to stitch up the giant otter's tail. Wrapping it with a splint and bandage took every scrap of gauze she had. Though she kicked herself for not bringing more—she'd known she was coming to see a *giant* otter, after all—Sunlit was satisfied with her work. In looking over the rest of Joy, she found scraped paws and traces of a near miss with a concussion. The otter, it appeared, was much tougher than her plush coat and light chitchat would indicate.

Next, Sunlit lured Biscuit down onto the pier, to feed him dinner and see if he was showing any signs of stress. They'd had a big day, after all. But the parrot seemed quite content, scattering seeds everywhere and complacently hopping onto her shoulder when she finally rose.

The third examination was of the boardwalk and beach. Both seemed deserted; it was now late into the evening. The shops along the boardwalk all had lights, of course, but it seemed that after a day of storm recovery, Seaside's citizens had gone home for a bit of recovery themselves. Even Officer Sabrina was gone, though Sunlit noticed a new "private" sign on *her* pier when she, Joy, and Biscuit made it back to the shoreline.

Then came the examination Sunlit was most worried about: the bait shop. Though she could stitch and wrap up just about anything, she had no experience in carpentry or roofing. Given the varied reports she'd heard about the bait shop during the day, she didn't dare get her hopes up.

She needn't have been *quite* so worried. Where the pier connected with the boardwalk, there was a sturdy plaza just above beach level, which sloped up from the waterline. The bait shop sat on the seaward side of this, perched just to the right as Sunlit and Joy walked down the pier. Though another large boat seemed to have been caught between the pier and the breakwater, miraculously its bow had not scratched the bait shop's wide windows. After a brief search, Sunlit found that the shop had a large side door that opened onto the pier as well as a front door that faced the rest of the boardwalk. The key Taiwo had entrusted her with earlier worked like a charm.

The door creaked on rusty, salt-encrusted hinges, but it opened, and all the anti-vandalism spells gave way to Sunlit and her key. It turned out that the side door, much like a barn door, could open in two parts—a top and a bottom; and by holding both open as far as they could go, Sunlit made enough room for Joy to pad into the shop.

The interior, fortunately for a giant otter, had been completely cleaned out. All that remained was a built-in sales counter at the far end and many, many cobwebs. Joy sighed gratefully as she eased herself over the well-worn hardwood floor. Though she'd not complained as they climbed over debris on the pier, she stretched out now and was asleep in seconds.

Sunlit remained rather more dubious. She'd kept her lantern handy, and now she shone it into every corner—half expecting ghosts or squatters, half expecting storm damage and rot. But the building, despite Officer Ebb's observations, seemed to be sound. The sales counter had been constructed in a large L shape around the corner, and behind it, Sunlit found another door and a ladder. The door opened rather abruptly out over the breakwater; it may have once been an entrance for sailors who'd tethered their boats at the old pier, but it was only good for a nasty shock now. The ladder turned out to be more useful. In a few cautious steps up, Sunlit could reach a hatch in the ceiling.

With a deep breath to calm her nerves, she pressed the hatch open. It gave easily, but the space beyond was pitch black. Sunlit extended her lantern cautiously, wondering if perhaps she should wait until morning—but in that moment Biscuit shook himself awake and leapt for the opening, squawking, "*Any port in a storm!*"

"Biz! Come back here!" Sunlit whispered, not wanting to wake Joy. This plea had no effect whatsoever on the parrot, which had disappeared.

Now, of course, there was nothing for it. Sunlit gathered up her courage and climbed the ladder.

She pulled herself into a sitting position, her legs dangling through the hatch. Her lantern illuminated an attic space that ran the length and breadth of the store below. The rafters were higher than she'd expected, and the flooring more solid. There were no holes, gremlins, or skeletons evident anywhere. Just a large blue bird perched above her head, looking smug.

"Well . . ." Sunlit let her voice fade away, swallowed up in the darkness. She wasn't sure whether to reprimand Biscuit or to be grateful. The attic could make a natural bedroom, but like the store, it had been left completely empty. Sleeping up there wouldn't be any more comfortable than sleeping on the shop floor below.

Just as Sunlit was mulling this over, a thunderous snore echoed from below.

". . . I guess that settles that, then," Sunlit said to herself. In one last examination, her briefest and most cursory yet, she realized that she, too, was very tired. After setting up her pack along the wall and changing out of her dirty clothes, without even eating her sandwich, she managed to stretch out and fall asleep.

4

A Delayed Start

The New West Key Azure is a parrot species known for its loyalty, brilliance, and uncanny conversation. As of this writing, many studies have been conducted on the Azure. Aside from the fact that it prefers oceanic shorelines and lives up to seventy-five years or more in the wild, very little has been ascertained. It remains an open question if the bird knows the meaning of the phrases it parrots . . .

—*from* Traverse's Guide to Marine Vertebrates, Invertebrates, and Magical Outliers

Sunlit woke early the next morning, full of plans (and pains from sleeping on uneven planks). Light streamed into the attic, which turned out to have more amenities than expected. First were the dormer windows looking out over the plaza, which— with a little elbow grease—opened to let in fresh air. Then, at the far end of the room, Sunlit discovered a rustic but quite functional private bathroom. She cleaned herself up as fast as she could and swung down the ladder to check on Joy.

The otter was stretched out on her back, taking up well over one half of the shop floor. She was sleeping peacefully, however, so Sunlit was pleased. Fortunately, Joy didn't seem to have noticed that Biscuit the parrot was snuggled into her fur, either.

"You're in charge," Sunlit told the parrot. "Stay here."

Its avian eyes watched her as she opened a few more windows, chowed down a day-old sandwich, and then let herself out the front door.

Sunlit, an early riser even at the best of times, was on the pier before anyone else that morning. The breakwater and new pier above bustled with activity, though. Sunlit navigated a stretch of boardwalk and a wide staircase to get to the marina just in time. She managed to buy some fresh seafood off the morning's first returning fishers with what little was left of her money. Feeding Joy was going to be a big task, not because of any special food needed, but because the otter herself was so big. Fortunately, Sunlit had spent an entire summer as an intern in the Marine Center's kitchens. The sailors supplied her with everything she needed, and also gave her plenty of suggestions about other places in town to visit for necessities.

After delivering her fish to the bait shop ice box, hidden under the sales counter, Sunlit made a trip to the post office to apprise Professor McAlpin of the news. Her letter ran something like this:

Dear Professor,

Arrived safely yesterday and saw to the otter. Minor injuries and a laceration. Some concern of infection, because it was left untended all day in unsanitary conditions. Otter was in good spirits—

Here Sunlit hesitated. She knew Joy had been in relatively good spirits, of course, because they'd been talking the entire time. But she had never gotten any kind of *feeling* from Joy—not like the feeling she'd gotten from Corduroy the clam, or any number of other sea creatures over the years.

But then, she'd never really understood those "feelings," and she certainly couldn't control when they came. So she shook the thought off and continued.

—but suspect adrenaline responsible for her liveliness. Still hope to be back for the conference, but may need more time for otter to recover. Especially if infection develops. Please send more gauze and antibiotic potion as soon as convenient.

Haven

P.S. In order to treat the otter, I had to purchase the pier . . .

Just writing the words made her feel incredulous.

. . . should I reach out to one of the admins at the Center to see if they'd mind taking it on as an outpost?

With a pit in her stomach, she sent it out. She may not have had semi-magical healing-related feelings, but she definitely had feelings of shame over imposing upon the University this way. But it couldn't be helped, she decided.

Sunlit knew it would be a while yet before Joy was awake, and she needed something to do to distract herself. Reading over the two reference books she'd brought for the millionth time was not going to cut it. She loitered in front of the little post office, uncertain. It was at the north end of town; surely, if she walked back through the town streets instead of along the boardwalk, she'd find something useful? An apothecary, perhaps, or a grocery market?

Sunlit set out. Her intentions were good, but the truth was, she hadn't been anywhere but New West Key since she was a child. She had none of the skills of a traveler, and all of the anxieties. Street names flew through her mind and out of it again. The local shop owners and the families that thronged the dusty streets were all jovial and friendly, but Sunlit couldn't imagine asking someone for directions. How would she explain herself? Where would she tell them she was trying to go?

In the end, she was hopelessly lost.

Cut off from the beach by several blocks of town, hidden from the sun by her big brimmed hat, she despaired of any chance at navigation. The streets back home were orderly, familiar—these were jumbled and full of distraction, a vacationing shopper's dream. Sunlit was just about ready to sit on a street corner and cry in frustration when she noticed that the building beside her was a bookshop.

Relief swept through her like a tidal wave. The bookstore, at least, was a familiar institution. All across Beyond, a network of scholars ran these centers: not only did they sell books, but they often looked after town records and local history as well. Sunlit was a frequent visitor at the one in New West Key, which was huge and home to several scholars, due to the proximity of the university. Seaside's bookstore was small and vaguely nautical in design, just another quaint shop, its windows full of beachy titles. But the font that spelled out "bookstore" across the door was unmistakable. Sunlit practically fell inside.

"Up here," a voice called, as the bells over the door jingled.

Sunlit paused to get her bearings. The first floor of the shop was entirely taken over by bookcases of novels, neatly labeled by genre. It might have been crowded or overwhelming, but for the clean white shiplap walls and occasional decorative signs boasting slogans like "sunrise, sunburn, sunset, repeat." This one in particular made Sunlit tug at her sleeves, but she knew it was meant to be cute and fun.

Crossing the thin carpet between the shelves, she found a staircase midway through the shop that led to a loft above.

A face peered down over the railing. "Want me to activate the elevator?"

"Oh, no, thank you," Sunlit said. "Stairs are fine. I'm just a little . . . new here."

"A lot of people are," the scholar observed. Her face disappeared as Sunlit climbed the stairs.

The loft, it turned out, served as both office and archive. Sunlit glanced around at rows of waist-high filing cabinets on one side, and the large desk tucked against the wall on the other. Skylights let in filtered light. It was common practice to charm glass to limit any harmful effects of sunlight, but Sunlit kept her hat on, just in case.

The scholar watching her didn't seem to mind. She was short and slight, leaning against her desk. Like all official "scholars," she wore long black robes, but her hood was thrown back to reveal violet hair and catlike ears over a tawny face. Large round glasses framed her almond-shaped eyes. Her chin and mouth were soft, neither approving nor disapproving, as if she was reserving judgment until Sunlit spoke again. She was, Sunlit decided suddenly, *very* cute.

"I'm Rachel," the scholar said. "Welcome to Seaside. This is your first time, I take it?"

Sunlit nodded, blushing. "I got a bit—well, to be honest, I'm lost."

Rachel glanced over Sunlit's boots, light overalls, and long sleeves. "Are you the researcher from New West Key University? So that wasn't just a story then, huh?"

"I, um, I'm just here to help a giant otter that was hurt in the storm. I don't know what else you might have heard," Sunlit said, not sure if she was mortified or flattered that this intelligent, poised scholar had already heard so much about her.

"Taiwo was in here last night talking about paperwork for the old bait shop, but I only half believed them." Rachel ran a hand through her hair, which turned out to be short and thick, flaring out over her shoulders in inviting waves. "Well! So if it's all true, you'll be staying a while?"

"A—a little while, yes," Sunlit agreed nervously. She didn't want to make any promises. But right now, staying didn't sound *so* bad . . .

"That's great." Rachel beamed at her, and Sunlit got the feeling that somehow, she'd passed a test. "We need some new eyes around here. Shake things up a little. So, what can I get for you? I don't actually have much about the bait shop itself right now, especially since Taiwo took the old blueprints and deed to present to the council as part of your purchase. I'm sure they'll be giving you those soon. But I can give you a town history if you like, to help you get settled. Or—"

"Oh, I don't need anything in-depth," Sunlit interrupted, unable to help herself. "I wasn't trying to give you more work to do. Only, I had a little extra time to do some errands but then I was lost, and then I saw your shop, and I thought . . ."

Rachel watched her as the words trailed off. Then, she smiled again, more gently this time. "Here's the plan. I'm going to loan you my favorite book on Seaside, and I'll give you directions back to the boardwalk, too. Okay?"

"Okay," Sunlit said slowly, distracted as Rachel grabbed a book from a nearby spinning rack and pressed it into her hands.

A Guide to Seaside (for the Discerning Tourist) was written in authoritative font across an antique map of town on the cover.

"You aren't exactly a tourist, but that's exactly the point," Rachel told her, matter-of-factly. "This has a much better history than any of the boring old town records, in my opinion. Give it a shot. And here, why don't you take this one, too?"

Spinning the rack once more, Rachel extracted a battered paperback that read *I'm an Adventurer Here, Myself,* scrawled across a rather dramatic image of a ship at sea.

"Oh, but—" Sunlit immediately started to protest.

"Just a loan, mind you," Rachel cut in. "You can see I loan it out a lot. You'll like it. Travel writing with a humorous narrator. I have an eye for people's preferred genres, you know."

"You—do?" Sunlit wondered, for a fleeting moment, if this was like the 'feelings' she got with animals. Then she shook the thought away.

"Call it experience," Rachel said, adjusting her glasses. "Now, if you want to get back to the beach, you're going to go out the front door and turn right . . ."

* * *

Following Rachel's directions was immensely helpful. Sunlit managed not only to get back to the bait shop, but to bring back a modest selection of groceries and some extra bandages and pills from the town's pharmacy, too. Joy was so large that any medication dose had to be suitably large to take effect. And while she was walking the streets with a little more confidence, Sunlit noticed that the town hall had set up a donation center where people affected by the storm could take a few comforts. Though at first she would not have considered herself a qualified candidate, Sunlit eventually allowed the man coordinating the scene to convince her to take a few things. By afternoon, the bait shop had a camp stove, tableware for two, a couple of old chairs, and a collapsible cot under a pile of blankets in the attic.

"If we leave soon, we can just donate everything back," Sunlit told Biscuit, over a belated lunch of grilled cheese sandwiches. "We're just borrowing it really."

But leaving soon was less and less of a reality in the light of day. Though Joy had responded well to being patched up the night before, she was asleep for most of the day, waking only to munch on a few mussels before dozing off again. The adrenaline that had kept her going before was nowhere in evidence now. Sunlit had learned in her studies that sometimes larger animals could sometimes take respectively longer times to recover, and she had a sinking suspicion that this would be the case with Joy.

As she changed out the bandage on Joy's tail and found signs of infection, she caught herself trying to get a "feeling" from Joy. How long would the healing process take? In the end, she walked away just as confused as before. Frustrated, she threw herself into chores.

"Okay. So we may be here a while," Sunlit eventually admitted to Biscuit. She'd scrubbed the shop clean, including a bit of vomit from Joy, and was feeling more grounded in her situation. Sitting atop the sales counter with *A Guide to Seaside* open in her lap, she felt less out of place, at least. "Going back for the conference was a pipe dream, maybe. But that's okay. We can make this work, and read those books from Rachel, and maybe help them clean up the pier . . . Or, I guess, we're the ones who technically should clean it up . . . Anyway, we'll be here maybe a week, just to make sure Joy's okay. It won't really be that long. But I don't like the look of that infection. Then we'll just have to sort things out with the university about this pier . . . I could donate it to them, maybe?"

"*We're the ones,*" said Biscuit.

"Yeah . . . thanks for that input." Sunlit shifted. From her perch, she could see Joy and also the boardwalk through the first floor windows. The sun was setting, casting a warm glow over curious faces as they passed by. Their searching glances made Sunlit want to hide under her blankets in the attic.

Just then, though, there was a knock at the side door. Sunlit had left the top half of the door open during her cleaning, and now a dark-skinned, shirtless man poked his head in.

"Sunlit Haven?" he asked gruffly, peering into the gloom of the shop.

His voice sounded a little familiar, but it still made Sunlit jump. "Back here," she called. "Wait a moment, I'll come out. Is something wrong?"

"You might say that," said the man as Sunlit made her way over, careful to avoid Joy's freshly bandaged tail. "We found someone."

"You found—some*one?*" Sunlit tripped over the words as she opened the bottom half of the door.

There, next to the man in swim trunks, stood a little boy looking up at her with ocean-blue eyes.

5

A Little Stranger

> *Myths abound regarding Seaside's founding. Some say a shipwrecked pirate hid his loot in the cliff caves nearby, but could never remember where, so eventually he had to build himself a home and spend his days searching. Others say the town's location was chosen specifically by a troupe of retired adventurers who wanted the perfect beachfront to settle. Still others say that one day, a forgotten clan of merfolk grew tired of the sea and walked up onto the beach . . .*
>
> —from A Guide to Seaside (for the Discerning Tourist)

"Hi!" the little boy said with enthusiasm. Sunlit had no experience with children. In fact, she'd grown up with her grandparents, and was most comfortable with people who had several decades on her at least. She tutored at the University, but only as a means to an end: helping more animals. As such, she got the feeling that *something* might be strange about this little boy . . . But she really couldn't put her finger on it. His head was smooth and bald, his ears small, his nose flat. But he didn't look like any kind of "kin" or sea creature she knew of, that was for sure. And he spoke easily. "Are you Sunlit Heaven? You can call me Fish. I'm a kraken! I made the pier get all messed up!"

"Oh," said Sunlit, with nothing but shock. She looked up at the man accompanying the child.

As if he was being asked why he'd returned the kraken to the scene of the crime, the man shrugged one broad shoulder. "He turned up on the beach. There doesn't seem to be any family around."

"But this is a marine sanctuary," Sunlit blurted out. "I mean, *this* isn't, yet, or at all, but I *work* at a marine center, and we've never had . . . chil-"

"I'm not a child," Fish interrupted, with lightning-fast acuity. "I'm a kraken."

"Well I've never tended to those either," Sunlit informed him, before giving the man a *please help me here* look.

"But you tend giant otters," Fish said, peeking past Sunlit's legs through the open door. "Is that a giant otter? Is it alive?"

"I have *so* many problems with this right now," Sunlit hissed desperately at the strange man. "Please tell me this isn't what I think it is."

"I want to ride the otter," Fish declared.

"Her name is Joy, and she's recuperating, so no one's riding her anywhere," Sunlit said without thinking. "Can one of you *please* tell me—"

A new voice entered the scene. From the direction of the new fishing pier, around the corner of the bait shop, someone called, "Oi, Professor!"

Sunlit could have cried in frustration.

Even more tempting was slamming the door shut and running. But because it was the barn-door half-open style, that would have taken too much time. Before Sunlit could move, Chip rounded the corner and caught them all. A large, dripping basket filled his arms. He was, of course, still talking. "Thought you might want some of the bycatch today for Joy. None of 'em are poisoned, you can trust me on that!"

The swimsuitted stranger turned and crossed his arms, glaring at Chip and his basket of fish. "Now I need to write you up for poisoning beachgoers, too?"

"No, I said there's *not* poison," Chip retorted. "What do you think, I'd poison something and then go around telling people about it? Hello to you too, by the way. And who are you, little friend?"

As Chip engaged Fish, Sunlit realized where she'd heard the strange man's voice before. This had to be Ige, the safety-conscious lifeguard who'd yelled at Chip the night before. Looking at him closely for the first time, she noticed the iridescent scales on his legs. Many merfolk could use magic to transform their tail into legs as needed, but often the scales remained. Ige's were such a deep blue that in the shadow of his red swimsuit they nearly blended with his dark skin. His head was shaved and his form muscular, but Sunlit felt his large blue-purple eyes were reminiscent of Taiwo from town council.

Town council—a much more appropriate place for a lost child.

The child in question was happily describing to Chip how

he'd destroyed the pier. Sunlit didn't want to miss her chance. She gave Ige a *what is going on here?* look again.

"He swam in at lunchtime," Ige told her quietly. "We've been looking for his guardians ever since. But if you ask me, they're still out there." With a motion of his head, he indicated the ocean behind him.

"And he *swam* in, but you never saw him swim *out?*" Sunlit whispered, so as not to disturb the aptly paired Fish and Chip. "Has anyone gone out looking for a boat?"

"Shipwrecks off shore aren't my job, but there's a network that looks after that kind of thing," Ige said, with a brief glance at Chip that conveyed that, as much as Ige might not want to admit it, the fishing boats probably did a good job of keeping an eye on one another. "Look, we sent word to the merfolk camp, to the marina, to the police, and to the council. But no one knows anything yet. He just needs—"

"Who's 'we'?" Sunlit interrupted, confused.

"Hasn't he shown off his badge yet?" Chip asked, abruptly joining the adult conversation. Sunlit realized then that he'd been listening all along: one fluffy ear was trained on them. "Ige's head of the Seaside Beach Lifeguards. No doubt they'll award him a medal and a deed to the town any day now."

"At least I *have* ambition," Ige growled.

"Is that what you call it? And yet look at which one of us is actually being helpful," Chip fired back, indicating his heavy basket of shellfish.

"Ige saved me," Fish said brightly. "He wasn't afraid of the *kraken!*"

The last word was announced in a surprisingly loud roar. People on the boardwalk turned their heads to stare before hastening on. Sunlit groaned as she heard Joy shift and mumble behind her.

"I need peace and quiet for my patient to recover," she informed Ige, disregarding the other strange strands of conversation. "Surely the lifeguards have some kind of a—club house or something, where he could stay? Or doesn't the town have, I don't know, a lost and found—"

"I think when it's kids they call them orphanages, Professor," Chip said helpfully. Then, unhelpfully, he looked down at Fish and added, "But you don't need one of those, do you, buddy?"

"I'm not a kid," Fish told him. "They don't allow not-kids there!"

Sunlit felt like the top might fly off of her head. No matter how much she stared at Ige, though, he remained impassive.

"No, we don't have one in town, to answer your question," he said with a shrug. "And the club house is for serious business."

"*I* run a serious business!" Sunlit protested, forgetting that she was trying not to run anything at all. Except herself, away.

"Hey, Chip, want to see what kraken business is like?" Fish asked.

"Always," said Chip.

"Look," said Ige, ignoring them both to focus on Sunlit, "you run a sanctuary, right? And it's right here on the beach. Close to where he was found. If we're lucky, we'll find his family any time now. And even if not, it'll only be for a few days while everyone decides what would be best to—"

Sunlit couldn't hear the end of the sentence. The sentence had no end, technically. As Ige was speaking, a small tidal wave exploded on Sunlit's doorstep, drenching herself and her visitors. Chip dropped his basket and shells went everywhere. Sunlit fell back against the door.

"Isn't kraken business *cool*?" Fish asked, eyes sparkling.

"And that," said Ige, water dripping from his face, "is why we can't take him to any old daycare."

* * *

Sunlit had thought to pack one towel, but only one. So she, Fish, and Chip sat in the sun on the old pier with their legs dangling over the side, waiting while Ige ran to the lifeguards' station. The boardwalk and beach were busy, faces bright in the evening sun. Sunlit hid under her big straw hat and worried, not least about the fact that she was letting Fish sit at the edge of a pier with no railing.

"If you think about it though, it does kind of make sense, Professor," Chip said cheerfully over Fish's head.

Sunlit looked down at the little boy between them, who was leaning over to peer at the water half a dozen feet below. Now that she was right next to him, she felt differently than before. He was very small and slight. He'd been short enough to hide behind the bottom half of her shop door, after all! He couldn't have been more than four.

His claims to kraken-hood had seemed silly at first, but now Sunlit wondered. Fish had no hair, and the ridges of gills were just visible beneath his tiny ears. His skin was an odd shade of gray—or at least, it had seemed that way in the shadow of the bait shop; now, in broad daylight, it seemed like it might be very pale blue . . .

Abruptly, Fish looked up at her with a big smile. "What's a professer?"

Sunlit hesitated. For a moment, his teeth had looked sharp, almost fang-like. But the moment passed.

"That's *Professor* to you, little buddy," Chip said for her. "It means Sunlit's the smartest one of all of us. Don't you worry—she'll know exactly what to do."

Sunlit resisted deep urges to bite her cheeks and shrink into her boots. Truth be told, if asked about life in general at any given point on any particular day, she'd have said that she had no idea what to do. But if Fish was truly in need of specialized help . . . Well, Sunlit knew exactly how to help those who'd been hurt or left by others. As far as she was concerned, that was her defining trait.

"I'm not worried," Fish told her. "I think it'd be fun to stay with you. Can I ride the otter?"

"If Miss Haven said no, that means *no*," Ige said from behind them. He dropped a towel on Chip's head, handed one politely to Sunlit, and then crouched next to Fish with an extra. "You don't really need this, do you?"

"Nope," said Fish, shining in his happiness. "I *like* water."

"You all don't have to keep calling me 'Professor' or 'Miss,'" Sunlit said, wrapping her towel around her shoulders. She couldn't quite recall having said *no* to riding the otter, but she was glad she had. "Just Sunlit or just Haven is fine. Either one."

"You didn't think we were calling you 'Professor' because we're scared of you, were you?" Chip leaned over to grin at her, his hair fluffed and standing on end from toweling. "It's alright, you have a nickname now."

"Maybe she doesn't want one," Ige reproved Chip. Turning to Sunlit with a similar—and slightly frightening—intensity, he added, "Just tell us what you *really* want to be called and we'll do it."

"Maybe she doesn't want you badgering her," Chip interjected. "She said anything is fine!"

Ige gave up on Sunlit for the moment and rounded on Chip.

"That is *not* what she said!"

"*Anything is fine!*" squawked Biscuit from the bait shop roof.

"You have a bird?" Fish turned to Sunlit with eyes as wide as saucers. "Wow. *Cool.*"

6

A Quiet Life

. . . Myths notwithstanding, Seaside can be a magical place, when considered in light of its history. The oldest part of town is undoubtedly the Rise estate, situated on the northern bluffs. However, the boardwalk itself, once a busy port, is the oldest part of the town proper. It didn't take long for early settlers to see its tourism value, and to shift their shipping and fishing industries further south. As of the writing of this book, the boardwalk is nearing its three hundredth anniversary as a beachy entertainment center and childrens' delight.

—*from* A Guide to Seaside (for the Discerning Tourist)

A delighted Chip insisted on taking Fish and Sunlit down the boardwalk for dinner that night. Though Sunlit still strenuously resisted the idea of settling into town or making ties, she found she *was* grateful not to be alone with Fish just yet.

It wasn't that Fish was unruly or excitable. In fact, for a self-proclaimed kraken, he was very mannerly. However, much as Sunlit tried asking him about his parents or family, her every question seemed to get her nowhere. Not to mention that strange things—like tidal waves out of nowhere—did seem to follow in his footsteps.

For example, after splitting an enormous tray of tacos between them, Chip and Fish had great fun playing boardwalk games . . . until the coin toss barrel suspiciously filled with water when they didn't win.

Sunlit did her best to apologize to the game owner while Chip led Fish toward the next distraction. "I really don't know how he does it," she confided. "I really am sorry—"

"Children with magical powers ought to be taught to control them," snapped the owner, tall and green-skinned and exasperated.

"We aren't really sure if it *is* magic," Sunlit hedged, forgetting more reasonable defenses like *he isn't my child* and *honestly, we can't be sure Fish did anything in the first place.*

"Looked like magic to me. And it's property endangerment either way," the game owner grumped.

"I don't know what to say," Sunlit said. *Coins are waterproof* might have been a good start, but she didn't say that, either. "I don't really have any money on me—"

"Just keep an eye on your kid," the owner demanded. "And good riddance to you!"

Feeling herself dismissed, Sunlit wandered off in shame and frustration. She found Chip and Fish a few shops down, lingering in front of a closed business. Fish had his nose pressed up to the glass.

"Chip says it's a *bakery*," Fish informed Sunlit as she joined them. "I want a cake pop!"

"I don't know if they even make those," Sunlit said, glancing at the cookie cutter–themed shop sign that read *Beachy Bakes.* "Besides, they're not open right now."

"Come back tomorrow," Chip told them both. "Arietta can make anything. And she can make it *look* like anything you want, too."

"We'll add it to the list," Sunlit said wearily. She knew from one glance at Fish's shining eyes that a straight-up *no* would get her nowhere.

Fish skipped on to the next stall along the boardwalk while Chip opted to keep Sunlit company. "She might have some good advice, too," he told her confidentially.

Sunlit found her head felt like it was full of seaweed. "Who?"

"Arietta. You'll like her. She can tell you where to get some new clothes, too," Chip added.

"New clothes?" said Sunlit, feeling vaguely like Biscuit. She picked at her long white sleeves. Had she gotten them that dirty already?

"Like, beachy things," Chip said, oblivious. "Might help you fit in."

Sunlit let the point slide. She didn't have too much interest in fitting in.

However, she decided, watching Fish dunk his whole head into a goldfish holding tank up ahead of them, *it might be good to get some kids' things.*

* * *

Sunlit woke the next morning with far fewer scruples about accepting donated furniture. After letting Fish take the cot and spending another night on the attic floor, she was sore in places she hadn't even known existed.

She got herself ready and went down to check on Joy as quietly as possible, but it didn't take long before Fish was scampering down the ladder behind her.

"The otter is awake!" he realized with rapture as he peered around Sunlit's side.

"Shhh," Sunlit insisted reflexively. But Joy, who was munching on squid with her eyes half closed, didn't seem to take notice of them. Sunlit went on, "She *is* awake, but she's—she doesn't feel good."

"Why not?" Fish squatted down so that his head and Joy's were on the same level, and watched her bite a fish in two with interest.

"She got hurt on the pier, and it's going to take her a while to get better," Sunlit said. She was so focused on trying to make sure she used child-appropriate words for things like "laceration" and "infection" that she forgot how Fish had taken responsibility for the wreckage.

"Oh, no," said Fish, very solemnly. "I'm sorry, Miss Otter. I didn't mean to hurt you."

Joy rumbled a bit and tilted her head.

"I'm sure she knows that," Sunlit hastened to say. Apologies weren't the usual prescription for infections, and she hated that Joy was already getting out-of-the-norm care, having to recuperate on a wooden floor instead of in a comfy aquatic center. "The best thing we can do for her right now is let her be quiet."

"But it's good to say sorry, right?" Fish asked, looking up.

"What? Oh—yes," Sunlit said, taken aback. "Yes, that was nice of you. So, um, with that done, do you want breakfast?"

"Is it fish bits?" Fish asked, staring at the empty basket beneath Joy's head.

"No. Unless that's what you normally eat?" Sunlit answered, uncertain.

"I can eat anything. I'm a shark. Do you know what sharks really like?" Fish asked as he stood.

Sunlit shook her head numbly.

"Sharks really like *cake pops!*"

She opened her mouth to say *they never taught us that at university*, but thought better of it. Instead, Sunlit agreed that the bakery was a good place for breakfast.

As they got ready to leave and locked up the bait hut, however, she wondered about Fish's new identity. *A shark, now? What brought that on?* Even more troubling was how much truth there was to any of these assertions. Sunlit knew a lot about caring for animals, but she knew next to nothing about people with animal characteristics or magical lineage. Such things were possible in Beyond, certainly, but she had no idea how it all worked. And while she was relatively certain that it wasn't possible to *change* one's heritage so easily, that still left her wondering what Fish actually might be. Normally she wouldn't worry about that kind of thing, but if he was going to go around conjuring water or potentially eating raw fish out of their tanks, that wouldn't be good for the sanctuary.

Wait—that's assuming I take on actual fish that need healing, too. Right now I don't even have a place they could go, she thought.

And no plans to stay, either. But all these quandaries found their way to the back of Sunlit's mind when she and Fish walked into Beachy Bakes.

It was open at this early morning hour, but just barely. Two small tables and wrought iron chairs had been set up beside the front window, along with a sandwich board that twinkled with magical lights outlining cookies and cakes. Hanging baskets full of bright yellow flowers on trailing vines framed the shop. Behind that big picture window, the shop itself was small—the front area could hardly have been bigger than Sunlit's attic bathroom. Nevertheless, another few tables and chairs stood along the walls, which were painted sky blue and decorated with fluffy clouds and colorful hot air balloons. At Sunlit's waist level, waves and sea creatures took over the decoration. A glass bakery case stood pride of place, rising up from the tiled floor and full to bursting with muffins, breads, and bars. A chalkboard listing out the options hung on the back wall.

Behind the counter, a gnome in a pale blue apron was sliding a tray of muffins into the glass case. She pivoted on her stool as they came in, smiling brightly over the register.

"I was wondering when you might come in," she declared.

Fish immediately had his nose to the bakery glass. Sunlit followed more slowly, focused on the gnome. She had wrinkled tan skin and a poof of blue hair streaked with gray rising above light blue eyes that matched her walls. Her voice was cheerful and matter-of-fact. Sunlit's, by contrast, was hesitant. "But I've only been here a day and a half, and Fish only just—"

"Oh, you'd be surprised how fast news travels here, dear," the gnome interrupted kindly. "Don't worry, you'll get used to it. And where are my manners? Please, call me Arietta."

"Sunlit Haven," Sunlit mumbled in response to this efficient introduction. "And this is Fish."

"Aren't you just," said Arietta, turning to beam down at the child—who, on an even surface, was probably as tall as she was.

"See anything in there that looks worth eating, love?"

"There's no cake pops," Fish said, looking up to Sunlit for confirmation of this terrible fact.

"Cake pops aren't really great for breakfast," Sunlit told him, somewhat relieved at the chance to introduce some mildly healthier food choices into the realm of possibility.

"That's true, I'm afraid," Arietta added, still smiling at Fish. "Maybe one day I'll make some. They could be cinnamon toast flavored, what do you think of that?"

Fish wrinkled his nose. "I never had cinnamon toast."

"Have you had a marionberry muffin? Those are my favorite," Arietta said, this time winking at Sunlit.

"What's a maronberry?" Fish asked.

He was hooked, and Arietta knew her business. She reeled in his interest with a professional touch, and took Sunlit's order of a croissant and slice of quiche while she plated the muffin. "I add bran and oats to the recipe," she informed Sunlit. Fish was busy testing the tables and chairs, finding them the perfect spot to eat.

"Ah," said Sunlit, reaching for her hidden travel wallet. It was very thin these days, but that was a trouble for later. "How much do I owe you?"

"For your first visit, nothing," said Arietta. Her eyes twinkled. "That's how certain I am that you'll be back. You have your pick of seats, don't you," she added more loudly, to Fish. "It's because you've come by so early. Do you mind if I sit with you, too? Otherwise I'm afraid I'll get bored behind this counter all by myself."

"Then you have to eat something too," Fish said, clambering onto a chair at the table in the front window.

"I'll be sure to bring something," Arietta promised.

In a moment, the three of them were seated, mouths full. Arietta had brought over a muffin for herself—and many other things, too; the table was suddenly full of baked goods, Sunlit thought. Not to mention orange juice and water.

"I can make tea, too, if you take it," Arietta said, wiping her mouth with a baby blue cloth napkin that sported an embroidered sugar cookie. "Most people on the boardwalk don't like it hot, but I do a good iced tea business in the afternoons."

"I would love some hot tea, actually," Sunlit admitted. She hadn't realized how much she'd been missing it. "But you don't have to get up. I could go and get it—?"

"Don't be silly, dear," Arietta told her. "I'll be back in a jiff."

And she was—after a few short clangs and bangs in the back room, that is. She returned to the table with a tray laden with three cups, loose leaf tea in little strainers shaped like seashells, milk, and honey. With great dedication and care, she quizzed Fish about his tea preferences. Sunlit watched this rather enviously. She wished she could be half as effective as Arietta was.

When Fish was settled with his "tea"—a mug of oat milk and a little hot water, mixed with a generous amount of honey— Arietta turned to Sunlit with a personable smile. Sunlit felt herself relax. In fact, she ventured to say, "Chip was saying yesterday that you'd be the person to ask about clothes and things?"

"Don't even bother with the boardwalk, not for yourself," Arietta began. "Unless you're *looking* for a bathing suit or a dress that's only fit for the beach, that is. If you want something sensible to work in, there's a consignment shop on Palm Street that's perfect. They have a tailor on staff, too. Our Fish may find something he likes there, or he may prefer boardwalk fashion. They grow out of it so quickly anyway," she added knowingly.

"He'll probably only be here a short time," said Sunlit, worried.

"Yes, well, and he can't go round in his bathing suit forever, can he? You're lucky my bakery doesn't have a dress code, young man," Arietta added to Fish teasingly.

"I like my bathing suit," Fish chimed in. His short legs swung beneath his chair as he devoured his muffin, smears of berry on his cheeks. "Ige gave it to me. It's good in the water!"

"He does have a tendency to get things wet," Sunlit confided in Arietta as she picked rather more demurely at her croissant. "But we'll take a look at that store—thank you."

"And what of *your* store?" Arietta asked, plainly curious. "Last I knew, there wasn't a stick of furniture in that old hut."

"There really isn't," Sunlit agreed. "But it's okay. I'm not really selling—"

"There's a giant otter in there," Fish proclaimed. "On the floor."

"As good a place as any," said Arietta, sensibly. "But surely not *all* of your charges can sleep on the floor?"

Just the thought of such a quarantine nightmare made Sunlit wince.

This was all Arietta needed. "I happen to know the owner of the consignment shop," she said. "Truth to tell, she started out in Seaside with this very bakery. This was ages ago, mind you, but I came on as her assistant, and when she felt it was her time to move on from baked goods, I bought the place from her. You'll never find a more reasonable business person. Anyway, the consignment store is her project now. I expect she likes the hours much better. But I happen to know she's been having the hardest time storing some of the things that come to her. Just last month, she had in an entire set of antique glass-front tanks."

Despite herself, Sunlit was fascinated. "The old Seafarer style, with shiplap siding and removable tops?"

"Wood and glass and the odd leak-proof spell, that's all I can tell you, dear," said Arietta, laughing. "I'm no kind of a professional like you. Only, I know Coral would *love* to get them out of her back room."

"They were made very sturdily," Sunlit went on, half unhearing. "And they have this modular construction that was really very clever for the time—"

"What's a moduler?" Fish interrupted, his muffin gone.

"Clean up your face, little love," Arietta said, handing him a napkin with a wink, "and you just may find out."

7

A Reclaimed Purpose

> *I don't know about you, but I like to let go and see where the wind takes me when I travel. Do what'll make the best story to tell the folks back home, that's my travel philosophy. You can't set sail halfway. We're all drifting through life hoping our dreams come true, so seize the chance and let them come!*
> —*from* I'm an Adventurer Here Myself

After they left Beachy Bakes, Sunlit and Fish's first stop was the little tourism booth at the northern end of the boardwalk. They were early enough that no one was inside, for which Sunlit was grateful. All she wanted to do was snag one of the rolled-up canvas maps of town from the storm-proof bin beside the booth's main window. She'd been too embarrassed to ask Rachel for one, and dreading the thought that she might have to go *back* to the bookshop for one. Fortunately, the information booth served her purpose (though she was just a *tiny* bit sad not to have to go back to the bookstore, after all). Now, happily, Sunlit had a map to point them to Palm Street. After her experience the day before, she wanted to be sure she knew where to go.

Sketched out in waterproof ink on sturdy canvas, the map was decorated with cartoonish landmarks and even a sea dragon, but the streets did seem to be drawn with precision. It showed Main Street running right behind the boardwalk, and then a number of side streets branching into neighborhoods and hotels. It even had a little hut marking the bait shop's location at the southern end of the boardwalk, and it showed the fishing marina as well as a neighboring cluster of homes labeled "Fisher's Village." Sunlit, of course, was most interested in tracing a path from the post office—set on the northern edge of town—down to Palm Street, set in the thick of downtown Seaside.

"Are you up for a long walk, Fish?" Sunlit asked, rolling up her map and sticking it in her deep back pockets.

"Sharks don't walk," Fish informed her. He'd been staring at the pictures of whale-watching cruises and parasailers plastered to the side of the tourism booth.

"But they do travel long distances," Sunlit countered. Usually for food, of course, but she kept quiet about that part.

Fish took to this idea naturally. "I can go *really* long distances!"

"Okay, good. But—" Sunlit hesitated. That *but* had managed to stop Fish from running off, but now she thought carefully about her next words. "But, even lone sharks know when to stick together, right? It's a big world out in the ocean. And it's the same here. There's so many people and streets and distractions . . ."

Fish considered her solemnly as her words ran out. Sunlit wasn't sure what to say next, how to get her point across.

But, fortunately, it seemed Fish had already understood her point. He walked back to her side and took her hand.

"See?" He said, swinging her gloved hand with his little one. "Now we won't get lost."

When they reached the post office, Sunlit was very pleased to find a package waiting for her—a battered, misshapen box stuffed to the gills with gauze, potion bottles, and a tube of vitamin capsules. That last bit made Sunlit smile: she always forgot to dole out vitamins, somehow, and it was one of Professor McAlpin's favorite things to tease her about.

But her smile faded as she saw that there was no letter in the box. *She's busy with the conference,* Sunlit reminded herself. But now, she had even *more* to report to her professor. She settled outside of the post office to write another missive. While Fish played at stuffing the tube and gauze back into the box, Sunlit wrote:

Dear Professor,

Thank you for the supplies. Everything proceeding as expected. Otter did develop infection and a fever.

Sunlit did waver over that last point. Joy's mouth was so big she'd nearly swallowed Sunlit's travel thermometer in a sleepy accident. She should ask her professor for another one, a larger and more reliable model . . . But then, she wasn't really setting up shop here, was she?

So far, though, infection is responding to treatment. Expect recovery soon.

Now, on to the trickier parts.

Town has asked me to look after a young boy. Seems to have ocean-related magic. Says he is a kraken? Is that possible??

Please advise.

Haven

P.S. I was thinking I would donate the pier to the university? There's a bait shop attached that would make a good Marine Center. It's small, but serviceable.

Rather than let herself ramble on, Sunlit folded up the letter and posted it, willing herself to move on. Fish was certainly ready to, in any case.

They followed their new map, Sunlit automatically guiding them to the shady side of each street as the morning sun rose. The streets in Seaside were hard-packed sand, with wide sidewalks lined by colorful shop windows and signs. The buildings were only one or two stories high, many with thatched roofs and brightly painted shutters. Though the town was clean and inviting, it wasn't quite as orderly as New West Key. Sunlit repeated the names of alleys and side streets to herself while Fish ran from one shop window to the next. *Tsunami Street, Hurricane Way, Seafoam Avenue* . . . The people of Seaside did seem preoccupied with storms, she thought. Coral's Consignment was tucked down an alley, a few blocks from the beach. Like Beachy Bakes, it was opening right as Sunlit and Fish paused by the front door.

"Did you tell them we were coming?" Fish asked Sunlit, looking up with wide eyes.

"No." After a beat, Sunlit smiled back down at him. "Maybe you're good luck."

It was a sleepy-looking teenager who opened the door— and quickly disappeared, leaving Sunlit and Fish to fend for themselves. They stepped into a store about the size of the bait hut filled with more things than Sunlit would have ever dreamed possible. Clothes filled racks and hung along the walls; in the corner by the front window, tidy shelves held toys and puzzles. Old wooden surfboards and brightly-colored linen beach umbrellas were visible at the back. Lanterns of every shape and description hung from the ceiling. Somehow, the chaos was inviting.

It certainly charmed Fish. He was immediately drawn to the toys in the corner. Sunlit left him with a quick *stay here, I'll be right back* before she made her way through the racks to find the sales counter.

"Hello," she said awkwardly to the obviously-disinterested teen. "Someone was telling me about some Seafaring tanks you might have here, and—"

"CORAL," the teen interrupted, rolling their eyes toward the lofty ceiling.

A woman emerged from a darkened doorway. With a few short words, she took her employee's place.

Sunlit was momentarily intimidated. Coral was tall and muscular, with tanned brown arms crossed over her yellow shift dress. Her black hair hung in braids down her back, leaving her wide face unobscured, her eyes such a dark blue that at first they appeared black. Despite Arietta's glowing recommendation, Sunlit found herself thinking about the door.

"You're here about the tanks?" Coral asked, her voice deep.

"Ah—that is—if you don't mind?" said Sunlit.

Coral scrutinized her for a moment, from long pants to boots and back up to her floppy sun hat. Then she tipped her head back and laughed. "Mind! At this rate, I'd pay *you* to take them. I can't get anyone else in Seaside interested. If they don't go with you, then I'll have to start using them to sort the clothes that come in."

"Oh, no," said Sunlit earnestly. "If they're everything Arietta was saying, then—"

"Arietta! I should have known." Coral smiled, looking suddenly very sweet. "Come on to the back, then, and see what you think."

In short order, Sunlit was in love. The tanks were everything she'd dreamed about as a child determined to start her own aquarium one day. And while those dreams had long since been set aside, the practicality of tanks that were waterproof, shatterproof, movable, and stackable was undeniable. Coral was willing to sell them to her on credit, and to throw in a few other necessities from the shop besides.

Sunlit returned to Fish to explain that he could pick out a few changes of clothes, only to find him engrossed by a wooden puzzle.

"Do you want that?" she asked hesitantly, thinking, *I only told Coral we want some clothes, but maybe*—

"No," said Fish. "Not that one. I want *this* one. Can I take it home?"

"Well . . ." Sunlit looked with some dismay at the box, which displayed a line drawing of a three-dimensional blue whale and advertised *five hundred interlocking pieces, all-natural colored rubber that will never break!*. It seemed like more than *she* could handle, much less a child of Fish's age. But the way he held it was endearing. "You can take it back to the bait shop, at least. When we find your parents, you can ask them about taking it home."

Fish hugged the wooden box and ignored the suggestion of parents.

"You have to pick out some clothes, too, though," Sunlit went on after a moment. "Arietta was right. We should at least get you a shirt and another bathing suit. And . . . shoes?"

"What if I wore long clothes like you?" Fish asked.

Sunlit gave up leaning over and sat down next to him, seeing that he wasn't ready to get up just yet. "You could do that if you wanted to."

"I don't want to," said Fish. He tugged at her sleeve as if to make sure it was really there and she'd really chosen to put it on. "Why do you?"

"Oh—well," Sunlit said, patiently holding out her arm, "ever since I was born, my skin burns really easily."

"Even if you went out for just a minute?"

"Even just half a minute."

"But why?"

"I don't know, Fish. There's a lot of things I don't really know about where I came from or what things were like when I was a kid."

"I don't know a lot either," Fish said, very calmly.

"That's okay."

"Yeah. What if you lived under a really big tree? Or in a cave? Wouldn't that be better?"

"I might not burn," Sunlit agreed, amused in spite of herself, "but I wouldn't be able to take care of animals like Joy."

"Oh," said Fish. He patted Sunlit's sleeve and smiled up at her. "Okay, I'm ready to go get clothes now. Can we get something that's gray? Did you know sharks are gray?"

"Of course I knew that," Sunlit said. "After all, you're gray, right?"

Fish smiled so big his eyes squeezed shut.

* * *

They got Fish outfitted in a little shirt and oversized sandals before stopping by the donation center again. As they returned to the bait shop with their box of mail plus another cot and a child-sized table for the attic, Sunlit found herself smiling.

That afternoon, just as Sunlit had finished a bit of tidying and Fish was happily scattering pieces of blue whale on the attic floor, another reason to be happy arrived. Coral had said she would have the fish tanks delivered, and she had quickly fulfilled her promise. Along with the tanks came Taiwo, bearing good wishes from town council.

"You've got the official stamp of approval from the council, and all your paperwork is here. And I've just heard all the latest updates," they assured Sunlit, handing over a thick roll of documents tied with twine and sealed with green wax. "Things are coming together, aren't they? I love it!"

Good, if everything is in order then the University has to do less, Sunlit thought, tucking the documents under her arm. Now that she wasn't distracted by a need to rescue an otter, she gave Taiwo a more careful look. The council person was effortlessly glamorous in a colorful wrap dress and large golden earrings. It was their wide smile and sparkling eyes, though, that really made Sunlit feel like she was about to be pulled into some sort of adventurous scheme.

And *that* made her think of her other responsibilities.

"What about Fish?" Sunlit asked, casting a glance at the attic windows. She and Taiwo stood outside the bait shop's front door; Sunlit had been politely but firmly kicked out of the way of the fish tank delivery, on grounds that she was slowing them down considerably and that *yes, we see the giant otter curled in the corner.*

"Inquiries have been made," said Taiwo, sounding rather

familiar. "But so far, nothing has turned up."

"He hasn't said anything about a family, or about growing up around here," said Sunlit, twisting her hands in her pockets.

"We have the town Witch on it," Taiwo said reassuringly.

But Sunlit was not reassured. She knew vaguely that to be a "town Witch" was a respected magical position, but she wasn't sure magic was *active* enough in this case. "Someone's got to be really worried—either that or—"

She didn't want to contemplate the alternative, and was glad when Ige strode up to them from the beach. "Any news?" he asked Taiwo gruffly.

"Hello to you, too, brother," said Taiwo.

"*Oh*," said Sunlit.

The pair looked at her.

She blushed. "It's just, I did think you had the same eyes, somehow . . ."

"Ugh," said Ige, as though sharing traits with his sibling was a burden too touchy-feely to bear.

"On that note, I must go," said Taiwo, eyes dancing in amusement. "Just wanted to stop by and deliver those papers. Glad to see how you're settling in, Sunlit. Toodle-oo!"

"But I'm not exactly settling—" It was no use. As Taiwo sashayed away down the boardwalk, Sunlit sighed.

"Why not?" Ige asked, eyeing her like she was a miscreant about to swim in prohibited waters at any moment.

"What do you mean, why not? I don't live here," Sunlit said.

"Technically, you are living here," said Ige.

Sunlit stopped and tilted her head to look up at him. She was beginning to understand why Chip found him so easy to argue with. "Anyway, Taiwo said they're still looking but haven't found any leads," she said, focusing on the matter at hand.

"That's what you meant by 'news,' right?"

Ige looked past her, to the consignment shop employees who still bustled in and out of the bait shop, each carrying a heavy fish tank. "What's all this?"

"It's fish tanks," Sunlit said, a little exasperated. "You all think this is some kind of fish hospital, don't you? Well, it isn't much of one if it doesn't have room for fish, does it?"

Ige looked back at her severely. "Do you ever smile?"

Sunlit gaped. It took her a moment to muster an answer. "Yes, I do, when I know that I've done my job well. And if you'll excuse me, my job right now is to make sure a giant otter and a boy-shaped shark are doing okay, and to see that the fish tanks all made it safely. So I'll just have to talk to you later."

And with that, she turned on her heel and fled into her little marine sanctuary.

8

A Leaky Pipe

Salt mites may appear related to fleas or other small insects, but unlike many of their brethren, they do not seek out living prey to feed upon. Instead, they make their homes out of evaporated salt, building tunnels much the way bees use wax. Until recently it was thought that they eat salt, also, but recent studies suggest that they survive upon calcium carbonate instead . . .

—*from* Traverse's Guide to Marine Vertebrates, Invertebrates, and Magical Outliers

It was in the quiet after Ige had left and the final fish tank had been delivered that Sunlit realized she didn't have an essential ingredient for her plan to work:

Water.

Of course, there was plenty of it around. The ocean was right outside her back door, quite literally (though a good half a dozen feet down, at the tide's highest point). Saltwater would be good for most of her charges, but ideally she'd want to filter it rather than bring it straight in from the sea. And even if she did bring it in, she'd be bringing it in by hand.

While the plumbing in the bait shop's attic worked just fine and brought in fresh water from the town's pipeline, the first floor was another matter. The sales counter seemed to have functioned as a working area in its former life: there was the ancient cash register, and of course the icebox tucked under the counter to one side. But set along the back wall behind the counter there was a wide sink, too, with two separate taps. The taps themselves did not confuse Sunlit; from her work at the Marine Center, she was familiar with the idea of having a sink that could provide both fresh and saltwater. For very sensitive creatures, or for the purposes of filling saltwater tanks, it was useful to have a saltwater tap. It made sense that a bait shop would operate on the same principles, so none of this seemed odd. No, what frustrated Sunlit was that neither tap seemed to work.

As she stood behind the counter staring at the uncooperative sink, she heard a thunking on the attic floor above.

"Sunlit?" Fish poked his head through the attic hatch. "My whale tail went everywhere. I can't find it."

"Huh?" Deep in her water-centric contemplations, it took Sunlit a moment to make sense of this.

"It bounced," Fish explained. "All the whale tail pieces. They bounced on the floor."

"Oh." Sunlit looked up, focusing on Fish and his new problem. "Don't lean over the door like that, it's dangerous. I'll come up and help you look in a minute."

Fish's head disappeared obligingly, but a second later, his

feet were slipping over the ladder on his way down. Sunlit stepped over to stand nervously behind him, guarding him from any fall. When he finally hopped down to the floor, he turned with a smile that indicated all whale tail bits had already been forgotten.

"Are you doing something?" he asked. "Can I help?"

"I don't think so," Sunlit said, as Joy snored in the back corner. "I'll come up and help with your puzzle in just a minute."

"But what are you doing?" As if led by instinct, Fish sidled up to the edge of the wide sink and peered in.

Sunlit sighed, and gave in to the inevitability of explaining. "Well, the new fish tanks will need water—most of them, anyway."

"What fish won't need water?" Fish interrupted.

"Not fish, exactly, but if we get any beach creatures—like a hermit crab or some kinds of snails—they might want just sand in their tank," Sunlit said. Fish accepted this thoughtfully, so she went on, "But I haven't decided how to get the water to put into the tanks."

"What about the sink?" Fish asked, as though he'd just discovered it himself.

"That *would* be good," Sunlit admitted, smiling in spite of herself. "But it doesn't work. See?" She reached over Fish's head, turning on one tap and then the other. All she got for her efforts were a rusty squeak and the sort of dusty cough that a blocked pipe makes as it tries, and fails, to fulfill its duty.

The noise attracted Biscuit, who had been investigating the empty tanks piled up in the middle of the shop. *"Drought! Drought!"* he croaked.

Fish glanced back at the parrot, his blue eyes interested.

"Sunlit, what's a drout?"

"Drought. It means there's no water from rain or streams or ponds," Sunlit said offhandedly, still thinking about her sink. "They don't really happen with seawater."

"Is there no water because the rain and streams are blocked?" Fish asked.

"No, usually it's a phenomenon due to weather patterns or over-use." Sunlit caught herself in university mode and shook herself back into the present, then thought more carefully about what Fish had said. "But the pipes in our sink might be blocked."

"They're blocked," said Fish, with confidence.

Sunlit looked down at his shiny head with some uncertainty. She'd seen him conjure water several times now. Did this inexplicable power extend to sensing the water around himself? It made a kind of sense, but she still couldn't figure out *why* the little boy might have that power in the first place.

"Do you want me to unblock it for you?" Fish asked.

Sunlit hesitated. "Do you think you could? How?"

"Like this." Fish held his hands out in front of him and screwed up his face in concentration. But since he was directing his efforts at Sunlit, not at the sink, nothing happened. Except a strange pulling sensation in her midriff . . . but that was probably just the nerves.

"Well," said Sunlit, because Fish was nothing if not determined, "in that case, okay. Yes, Fish, I'd love it if you could unblock the sink pipes, please."

"Cool!" Fish turned to the sink, bouncing up on the balls of his feet. "See, look, I can help!"

And with those words, he held his hand out to the freshwater tap. At first, nothing happened. Then there was a rumble.

Then, with a sudden shudder and the stink of old seaweed, the pipe ejected a green jumble of algae down into the sink. Water followed, spitting and gushing and finally running cool and clear and fresh as could be.

"Wow, Fish!" Sunlit tested the water, laughing with the sheer surprise of it. "You really did it!"

"I did!" Fish grinned up at her. "But I can't do the other one. It's blocked too far away."

"Too far, huh?" Sunlit wasn't about to let something like that stop them. Emboldened by their success so far, she opened the cabinet under the sink and took a look at the pipes. The freshwater one ran down under the floor, but the saltwater tap went straight out the wall. Sunlit sat back, satisfied. "I have an idea, Fish. Want to come outside with me for a minute?"

Of course, there was nothing Fish wanted more. But rather than climb out the back door that led to thin air, Sunlit took them out the side. She was so excited she almost forgot to grab her sunhat and lock Biscuit inside. But in the nick of time, she did, and from there they went down onto the beach. Even though it was nearing dinner time, there were crowds of sunbathers, ball players, and swimmers. Sunlit spotted Ige atop the red-and-white lifeguard stand midway down the beach. She avoided eye contact, not knowing if he would approve of what she was about to let Fish do.

She ushered the little boy with her, turning a tight lefthand corner to sneak under the pier. At its closest, it was only a foot or two off of the sand, but nearer the water, it was tall enough for an adult to walk under it easily. Sunlit and Fish ventured under it near enough to the bait shop that Sunlit had to bend halfway over. But she was too excited by the possibility of a seawater tap to waste time going down further.

When they emerged from under the pier, there was just barely enough sand to stand on. To their right, toward the sea, there was a wrecked boat wedged between the pier and the breakwater. The breakwater itself was only a dozen feet away. Sunlit knew she'd have to deal with that wrecked boat sooner or later—it was wedged in, but not so tightly that it couldn't be moved, which meant it might be a danger in future storms. That, however, was a trouble for another day.

For now, they turned their attention left, to the edge of the boardwalk above them—and the back of the bait shop above that. Looking up, Sunlit could easily spot where the pipe from the sink came out of the wall. It ran down along the back of the shop, then bent and tucked under the boardwalk before running straight down into the sand below.

Sunlit and Fish walked over to where the pipe disappeared into the ground, considering it.

"I've seen things like this before," she told Fish. "It probably has a spell on it that repels sand."

"But how does it get water?" Fish asked, turning over his shoulder to look at the waves. At mid tide, they were many feet away.

"Even though the sand feels dry to us, there's still water in it if you dig deep enough," Sunlit said. "Maybe the pipe draws water out from very deep. Or, maybe it goes down a little way, and then turns sideways and goes out nearer to the water. Can you—" She bit her cheek, wondering at herself for being about to ask such a thing: "Can you tell where it goes?"

Fish stood stock still with his head to one side, solemn and quiet. Sunlit waited. This was worth waiting for, in her opinion. Sand was a natural filter, and saltwater drawn up to the shop *through* the sand would need far less treatment before it was ready to be used. It was actually quite ideal for her new fish tanks.

And, of course, a clean saltwater tap would be a great boon for the University, if they decided to start a Marine Center outpost here.

"I can't see how far it goes, Sunlit," Fish said. His voice sounded thin, a little distressed. "I'm not big enough."

"Not big enough?" Sunlit repeated, feeling like Biscuit. Then she shook her head. "Well, it may not matter where exactly the pipe goes, Fish. What about where the block is? That's what we really need to fix."

"That would still be helping?" Fish lit up. "I can do that! I know where it is. It's right here."

He gestured toward a section of the pipe level with Sunlit's knees. She knelt to look at it, but could see nothing out of the ordinary. It was rusted, true, and weather-beaten, but otherwise looked perfectly fine. "Do you think you can fix it like you did the other one?" she asked.

"It's bigger," Fish said, "but I think so. Watch!"

Sunlit did watch, very carefully. But just like last time—like every time Fish had used magic—there were no warning signs. There was no theatrical waving, no sparkles or shines, no whispered incantations. There was just a little boy holding out his hands, his face screwed up as he concentrated. And then, faintly, a *pop* and the sound of rushing water.

"I did it!" Fish declared.

"I think you did. Let's go up and check," Sunlit replied, grinning. "I wonder what was blocking the pipe this time?"

"Let's go see," agreed Fish. He took her hand as they headed back under the pier, creeping close to the sand. Sunlit felt her heart swell.

But when they emerged back into the bright light of the beach, there was a shadow in front of them. Sunlit stopped short, one hand to her hat as she reeled. As she unfolded to her natural height, she found she had to look down slightly at the person who'd been waiting for them.

It was Sabrina, the junior officer who'd stood sentry by the pier on Sunlit's first night.

"We had reports of people sneaking around the pier," Sabrina explained, clearly a little taken aback by Sunlit and Fish's sudden appearance.

"That was just Fish and me," Sunlit said. "At least, we didn't see anyone else. We were just investigating some plumbing from the bait shop."

"Oh, right. I heard about you," Sabrina said, smiling down at Fish.

Fish beamed back. "I fixed the pipe!"

"Did you really?" Sabrina glanced at Sunlit, then to the pier behind them. "It's all your property now, so no harm done, anyway. As long as you two are okay?"

Sunlit held tight to Fish's hand, looking over the junior officer's uniform and little brimmed cap. It looked hot and uncomfortable—but then, Sunlit's own work attire probably looked much the same. She did wonder, though, if Sabrina minded having to come out and check on them.

"We're fine," she said at last. "Actually, we have something to check on, up in the shop."

"Well, don't let me keep you." Sabrina broke into a smile, waving a hand tipped in shiny pink nails today. Just as Sunlit was herding Fish up the beach, she added, "Oh, Miss Haven?"

Sunlit stopped, and Fish looked over his shoulder. "She says to just call her Sunlit," he informed the police officer helpfully.

"Okay then. Sunlit," said Sabrina, "I just wanted to tell you, all of us at the police station think it's really great, what you've done."

"For Joy?" Sunlit asked, confused.

"That too," Sabrina said. "But mostly I meant, looking after Fish, here."

"Oh!" Sunlit nodded out of habit, but was too surprised to say more.

Sabrina tipped her hat to them and left cheerfully. As she did so, Sunlit let Fish pull her up to the bait shop to check on the sink.

And when they walked into the shop to find water rushing from the tap, clearing out rust and remnants of salt buildup, Sunlit wondered if it really was a great kindness or favor that she'd done the town by taking in Fish . . .

. . . Or if perhaps Fish himself was doing her a favor by staying.

9

An Unexpected Parade

> *It is of tantamount importance that every animal be given its own specific and secure space. A feeling of security is essential to recovery. An animal stressed by sharing its quarters with a stranger, or by quarters unsuited to its preferred habitat, will take twice as long or longer to recover—if indeed it recovers at all.*
>
> —*from* Standard Practices for a Safe & Sanitary Animal Medic

The next morning, Sunlit was feeling decidedly better about the world. Sleeping on a cot, even an old and thin one, had helped considerably, of course. And the fact that she'd relaxed before bed with the travel story Rachel had recommended didn't hurt . . . in the course of her studies, Sunlit had become so accustomed to reading reference books that she hadn't considered reading something as conversational as *I'm an Adventurer Here Myself* in years. Why, it was practically fiction. And yet, Sunlit found it quite compelling. She could relate to that feeling of being a constant stranger. But she also found herself less frustrated with life in Seaside in general.

Part of that was because she'd fully embraced her purpose. She had Fish help her conduct a thorough check up of Joy, holding the free end of the otter's tail while she redid the bandages; and she used Joy as an excuse to get Fish to actually wash up and *wear* his new shirt. For her part, Joy seemed as tired as ever, but her infection was receding and she took some interest in the little boy. Seeing this, Sunlit decided that the two "patients" might really be good for each other after all—provided Fish didn't carry out any sudden, watery explosions. It wouldn't *hurt* Joy, of course, but the shock couldn't be good for healing. Fish proved to be a very dedicated nurse, watching over Joy very carefully as Sunlit tugged her new fish tanks into some semblance of order along the shop's front wall. It was hard work, but satisfying.

A quick walk to the post office revealed no new mail waiting for them . . . But Sunlit shrugged it off, determined not to let Fish see her down. Instead, as they wandered back down the boardwalk, she took the chance to ask him about his family again.

"Is there anyone that might send *you* mail, Fish?" she began.

"You would," he told her, pulling his gaze from a stall full of brightly colored beach balls that were *guaranteed to return to owner!* by the banner strung across the shop's front.

"Sure," Sunlit agreed. Because how could she say otherwise? And really, she wouldn't mind keeping up with a few people in Seaside once she went back to New West Key. Rachel might have more book suggestions, after all. "But do you think anyone out there is worried about you?"'

"You are," Fish said cheerfully.

"I am not—" Sunlit sighed. She'd never been a good liar, and she knew it. "I am a little."

"Look what I can do!" Impervious to worry or anything else, Fish beamed up at her, a ball of water between his little hands.

"That's cool," Sunlit assured him, though she couldn't help but think that the boardwalk was getting too crowded for magic tricks. "But maybe—"

Fish wasn't looking where he was walking. A deathly pale lady under a beautiful parasol tried to avoid him, but it was too late. Fish's beach ball of water splashed all over her fluttery, fancy summer dress.

Fish was waiting a few steps away and eager to walk on by the time Sunlit managed to assuage the lady, who turned out to be on town council with Taiwo. Sunlit made her effusive apologies and escaped as quickly as she could. She noted to herself that perhaps it wasn't so bad that Taiwo was the town representative most interested in the bait shop-turned-sanctuary . . .

"We have to be more careful, Fish," she said, as they resumed walking.

Fish did think about this, but it was clear he did not understand. "But water doesn't hurt."

"Sometimes it does," Sunlit told him. "If there's too much water, it can move things around, like what happened to Joy."

"I happened to Joy," Fish reminded her.

Sunlit glanced at the strollers and families around them, hoping fervently that no one was paying them any attention. A glare from a nearby police officer resting beside their bicycle did not reassure her in the slightest. "But a big wave could have done it, too," she said, a little desperately. "And some people don't like water."

"Why would they not like water?" Fish asked, curious.

"It depends," Sunlit said. "Maybe they think it's messy, or it doesn't feel good on their skin. You never know until you ask, Fish."

"*Until you ask!*" Biscuit squawked nearby, making Sunlit jump. They'd neared the shop, and she looked up to see the parrot perched in the attic window looking down at them.

"Is that what professers do?" said Fish. "They ask?"

"Um . . . Yes," said Sunlit, though she felt strangely uncertain. She thought again about her unusual feelings. She'd never actually asked the animals, in those cases. The knowledge just came. But should that really be the way it worked?

"I'll ask," Fish decided solemnly.

Abruptly, Sunlit was reminded of what *she* had been trying to ask. "Fish, who taught you things like this before you came here? Do you miss anybody?"

"I miss the ocean," he told her earnestly. "Can we go swimming?"

Far too worried to let him play by the pier, and leery of joining the tourists teeming the beach, Sunlit redirected him by promising to help put together his whale puzzle. It was, as she had suspected, much more difficult than many of her college classes had been.

By mid afternoon, Sunlit and Fish sat on the side door step so that they could watch the beach as they ate their lunch. Joy rested comfortably behind them, still exhausted from fighting her infection, but beginning to take notice of the world once more. Her head lay atop her paws nearby in case Fish had any otter-approved leftovers. Seeing as lunch consisted of apple chips and peanut butter and banana sandwiches, this was unlikely.

"*Home port calling,*" Biscuit squawked from some of the old pier's collapsed railing nearby.

"Want a banana?" Fish asked the parrot in return.

Biscuit did, in fact, want a piece of banana, and fluttered down to the doorstep to take his due. Sunlit continued looking thoughtfully at the old pier. "I guess we'd better clean it up somehow," she mused aloud, though mostly to herself. She didn't relish the thought of venturing out in the heat—the shade of the bait shop door was perfect, as far as she was concerned—but it *was*, technically, her responsibility . . . She even had the paperwork now to prove it.

"I'm sorry I made it break," said Fish.

"I—You don't—" Sunlit swallowed her protest as she turned to the little bald head, reminding herself of their conversation about apologies. "I appreciate you saying that, Fish. But it's okay, really. I—I forgive you."

She also still was not sure she believed Fish was the real culprit, but that was another matter.

Fish nodded gravely over the remains of his sandwich. "I'll fix it!"

"Um . . ." Sunlit shook her head, but she smiled, too. "How do you plan to do that?"

"I'll be an octopus with lots of arms," said Fish. Biscuit hopped nearby, hoping for another banana.

"Don't krakens have lots of arms, too?" Sunlit heard herself ask.

"Yes but those arms aren't for *building* things," Fish told her, with an air of, *everyone knows that.*

"Oh," said Sunlit. "Well, that's probably a good idea then. I could help too. Even though I only have two arms . . . sometimes I do *wish* I had more, though," she added whimsically.

"Then why don't you?" Fish asked, innocent.

Sunlit was just trying to sort out what he meant by that question when she noticed another child headed their way. Unlike Fish, though, this one was tall and lanky, perhaps twelve, a tan and sandy-haired boy that she could have sworn she'd seen around the boardwalk before.

"Is this the Marine Sanctuary?" he called as he approached.

Sunlit hesitated, only to find that Fish was also abnormally silent. Not wanting him to feel worried, she said more cheerfully than she felt, "That's right! Is something the matter?"

The boy drew up level with them on the boardwalk and held out a wooden bucket painted green. "I found this!"

Fortunately, Sunlit was more accustomed to bare statements of fact these days, with Fish for company. She didn't bother wondering what the child wanted or if she should say something about it, and instead poked her head over to take a look in the bucket.

Inside the handy pail was a lump of sand and a *very* large snail. Its snaily body glistened, a healthy orange, while its shell rose up in shiny purple spirals. Along the side, though, there was a large hole in the shell, as though the snail had taken the crustacean equivalent of a spear to the gut.

"*You* didn't do that, did you?" Sunlit asked before she could think better of it.

"Of course not," said the boy, affronted. "I found 'im that way. Took 'im to the lifeguard, but the lifeguard said best bring it here."

"Oh, is that so?" Sunlit pondered the snail. Fish, emboldened, pressed his head up to take a look too. Thinking aloud, Sunlit went on, "Well, it looks like a pretty healthy saturn snail to me—aside from the damage. He'll be able to repair it himself in time, if he's given a quiet place and lots of sand to use."

"Why's he a saturn snail?" Fish asked.

"Normally, saturn snails use their own kind of magic to make rings of sand float around them," Sunlit said, unable to resist the chance to talk about sea creatures. "This one has one, but it's very faint. See?"

She pointed out the hazy circle orbiting the snail's shell, and both children leaned in. But their visitor wanted more than a biology lesson, that much was clear. The boy kept looking at her expectantly—and then out at the beach, which was positively brimming with sunbathers and swimmers on this lovely day. Sunlit bit her lip. She saw where this was headed. But snails of all kinds were notoriously slow healers, slower even than a giant otter might be expected to be.

"He'd like a fish tank better than a bucket," Fish observed. "Then he could have a really big ring."

"Technically he'd like the *beach*, but I guess it's true that our tanks are big enough, and a lot more quiet than the shoreline here," Sunlit admitted.

"So you'll take him?" the boy asked, holding out the bucket and giving it a shake.

"We'll take it," Sunlit said quickly—if nothing else, to preserve the snail from further damage.

"Take the bucket too! *Yuck*, snail slime!"

Sunlit found herself with a bucket in her lap as the boy scampered back to his sand-castle building. Fish dropped the rest of his apple chips to take a look. Biscuit reappeared and began cleaning up the mess.

"Welcome, I suppose," Sunlit murmured down to the saturn snail. His ring kept spinning, caught in the snail's tiny magnetic field, but the snail took no notice of her. And try as she might, she could get no feeling from him.

"You know how to fix him, Sunlit? You're going to fix him here?" Fish asked.

"I know about helping animals heal," Sunlit admitted. "And animal care is animal care, no matter where you are. Even if it's just an old bait shop like here."

Whether the thought was encouraging or discouraging, she wasn't entirely sure. But Fish apparently wasn't worried about such nuances.

"Can I pick which tank he lives in?" he asked, eyes glued to the snail.

"Sure. The sooner we get him into a bigger habitat, the better," Sunlit said, inspecting the sides of the bucket. The paint did not seem to be flaking off, at least. "How about you pick the right one and I will put him in?"

They accomplished this easily, and Fish accepted a commission for more sand. As he raced out the side door with the empty bucket in hand to fulfill his quest, he nearly knocked over another visitor.

"Sorry about that," Sunlit said, bringing up the rear. She'd intended to keep a watchful eye on Fish, but found herself confronting a rather harried-looking woman with a baby in one arm and a large mixing bowl in the other. "Can I help you?"

"I had to wait until they were out at swim lessons," the woman said breathlessly. Frizzy red hair framed her face, pale pointed ears just poking out from the halo. She was tall enough that she could have been leaning down over Sunlit, but instead she seemed to sag all the way along her spine, as though exhaustion had taken its toll repeatedly. "You have to take them. I'm just at my wits' end. Can you tell us what's wrong? I'll fix it, whatever it is, but it may take me a few days. A few days is alright, right?"

"Um," said Sunlit, carefully unpicking all these questions in her mind. "Take who? Or—what?"

"These," said the woman. She thrust out the mixing bowl, causing water to slop over her arm and Sunlit's hand. Inside, just barely, were two long-finned, rainbow-colored fish, each about the size of a plum. "Spick and Spann, those are their names."

"Oh dear," said Sunlit, not so much about the nomenclature as the obvious droop in the fishes' scales. "I do think I'd better take them."

"You're saving my life," said the woman with a hearty sigh. There were deep circles under her green eyes. "Take the bowl, too. Do you need me to sign anything? I'll come back and pick them up in a few days. Can I pay you then?"

The baby started fussing in its mother's arms, giving Sunlit a quick moment to herself. *Pick them up? Pay?* Slowly, she realized that this mother had assumed that the new "Marine Sanctuary" in town didn't just take in wild animals, but functioned as a sort of hospital for tame ones.

And, well—why shouldn't it?

"That'll be fine," Sunlit said haltingly.

"Are you sure? I'd be forever in your debt," the mother said, shouldering her baby with a grateful smile.

"Yeah, no problem," said Sunlit. "Don't worry—I'll keep an eye on them. We'll be sure to remember you. Right, Fish?"

Fish, who had skidded to a halt—sandy bucket and all— beside Sunlit's legs, looked up and scrutinized the new lady.

"I'll remember! Octopuses are good at remembering."

"Perfect. Then I'll see you soon," the woman promised, beaming at both Sunlit and Fish before rejoining the bustle on the boardwalk.

"We just got two more patients," Sunlit said, more for her own benefit than for Fish's. "Want to see? Just be careful. I think they might be stressed out from too much noise and activity."

"Ac-tiv-ity," Fish echoed, taken with the sound of the word. He peered at the fish and directed them to their new home-away-from-home in the tank beside the snail.

"Two in one day," Sunlit mused, watching Fish dump sand into the snail's tank. She leaned on the sales counter with the now-empty mixing bowl on the counter beside her. In a moment she'd get up to get the fish more water; normally, she wouldn't have even stopped to rest until their tank was full. But the shock of being totally in charge of three new lives was wearing a little on her. Even at the university, there had always been someone to report to or to double-check, a wall of books to turn to, a professor to go to with questions—

"Knock knock? Hello?" called another voice from the front door.

"Hello?" Sunlit called back, confused.

Two muscled silhouettes paused at the threshold before entering the shop. As they left the bright sunlight behind, their forms resolved into those of two teenage lifeguards, one a girl with a plume of yellow Biscuit-like feathers rising from her head and one a boy with orange skin. Both wore the red uniform wetsuits of the lifeguards.

And each was carrying a large crate.

"This is Marine Sanctuary, right?" the first one asked.

"Yes," said Sunlit, cautiously.

"Hi!" said Fish. "Do you have patience for us?"

"We got patients, kid," said the second, grinning crookedly at Fish before focusing on Sunlit. "We *were* taking care of them down at the lifeguard station, but . . ."

"It wasn't really working," said his companion, matter-of-factly. "So when Ige told us about this place, we figured . . ."

"You'd better take over," the boy concluded. He walked over and rested his crate on the counter beside Sunlit.

Before she ventured an opinion, Sunlit grabbed her portable lightstick from beside the register and lifted the lid just an inch, peering in. Something skittered. Two reflective eyes blinked.

"A crab and a salamander?" Sunlit guessed, looking up.

"There's a couple clams in there somewhere too," the boy said sheepishly.

"Someone on the beach dropped 'em off last week saying they'd been cursed," the feathered girl explained helpfully. "But we never noticed anything, right?"

"Never," her partner confirmed. "But we kept 'em just in case."

"And the crab's missing a pincher. We found it in the storm debris," the girl added.

"And the salamander got its tail caught in a sand castle collapse in the storm, too," the boy concluded, not to be outdone. "We nicknamed it Iggy."

"Okay." By now, the thoughts were coming quicker. It was like a knack coming back to her. Sunlit's first priority was to separate the animals, but she didn't want to miss out on anything the lifeguards knew. She fished in the drawer under the register for a pad of paper. "Do either of you have a pencil? I want you to write down when you picked up each animal, where, and what happened to it, as best you can. Fish and I will get them settled."

"What's in the other box?" Fish asked, excited.

"Oh, this is supplies," said the female lifeguard, patting the wooden lid.

"We thought, we don't have money really, but maybe you could use some sunscreen potion and water pouches," the boy explained.

"You can keep all of it," his fellow declared.

"Thank you," Sunlit said, more out of habit than anything else. "We can leave that there, then. Fish, how about you help me pick three more tanks? And I'll need you to get us some more sand here, too, in just a minute."

"Octopuses get lots of sand," the little boy declared, swinging his green pail.

When next Sunlit paid attention to the lifeguards, they were handing her the information she'd requested, scribbled across three pages of note paper. *Perfect*, she decided. She could tack each paper to its respective tank.

And they were looking at her with identical smiles. "Nice place you got here," said the first.

"Is that an otter?" said the second.

"Tell me something first," Sunlit decided. "It was Ige who told you to bring everything here?"

The lifeguards looked at each other and nodded in unison. "He said you needed the company!"

10

A Fisher's Reprieve

Salamanders exist in many varieties. Most well-known is the fire salamander, perhaps, but the oceanic salamander is no less interesting. Equally at home on the sand and beneath the waves, it is one of those few creatures who represent a bridge between habitats. Though its belly is often described as "plump" by those unfamiliar with the species, educated scientists generally agree that this roundness is a result of the fact that the oceanic salamander has two sets of lungs. Its scales form patterns of yellow, green, and blue, and are much sought after by practitioners of ocean magic . . .

—*from* Traverse's Guide to Marine Vertebrates, Invertebrates, and Magical Outliers

Ige wasn't the only one who thought Sunlit's new sanctuary could use some improvement. That evening, Chip turned up with an enormous carpet roll over one shoulder.

"Someone's at the door!" Joy yelled from her place on the shop floor.

Sunlit and Fish both raced to be the first downstairs. Fish won, but only because Sunlit paused to turn down the heat on their camp stove. They'd been cooking noodles for dinner, and Fish was a little *too* interested in the boiling water.

When she finally hopped down the ladder, she saw Fish guiding Chip in through the side door. The carpet roll on the sailor's shoulder was nearly as long and fluffy as Joy, who remained flat on the floor.

At least she's more aware of her surroundings, Sunlit thought.

"Someone's feeling better," Chip said cheerfully, echoing this sentiment as he caught sight of Sunlit behind the counter. "Nice to see you, Joy!"

"Hello, food man. Don't step on me," Joy said, before letting her eyes drift close again.

"It's harder now that there are fish tanks by the wall," Fish observed. "There's not as much space."

"We have the space we need," Sunlit said. The thought of complaining or being ungrateful made her shoulders tense. As Chip swung sideways and nearly hit the wall with his carpet, she added, "Normally, at least. We don't usually have such large . . . um . . . what is that?"

"Chip brought us a carpet!" Fish declared helpfully. "I'm leading him where to go. Watch out, Sunlit."

As the little boy guided him—about as effectively as a tugboat willing a barge into place with just a pinch of magic rather than actual ropes and chains—Chip grinned at Sunlit. "Just a rug, really, Professor. Wait 'til you see it. It's exactly what you need. We used to have it in *our* attic, but Pa and I decided, what good is it doing there?"

"That's really . . . kind of you," Sunlit said. She wasn't sure a thick rug *was* what her attic needed.

But then again, it could come in handy for catching rubber whale parts.

"It's nothing," Chip assured her. "Help me haul it up the stairs, will you?"

With Sunlit pulling from above and Chip pushing from below, urged on by Fish, they managed to get the rug up onto the attic floor before sunset, at least. By the end, Sunlit's shoulders were aching and she was sure she'd inhaled a dangerous amount of dust. But when Chip and Fish unfurled the rug to reveal a woven ocean floor panorama, she had to admit it might have been worth it.

"It's so *cool!*" Fish cried, clapping his hands together.

Chip stood with his hands on his hips beside Sunlit, catching his breath. "Pa always said it was a bit too *on the nose* for a sailor's house," he confided in her, grinning. "But I loved it when I was a kid, too. It grows on you."

"It's certainly detailed," Sunlit said, looking down at woolen crabs and schools of yellow fish cavorting over slightly faded sand. "And it'd be a good place for Fish to play."

Fish himself was still in raptures. He knelt on the rug, hands disappearing in the heavy pile, exclaiming to himself over each new creature he recognized.

"I spent many a stormy day on the same rug," Chip said fondly. He didn't mention the fact that Fish was meant to be a temporary resident of the Sanctuary—as were they all, in fact. Sunlit was secretly a little relieved. As Chip looked around, he saw the table and whale puzzle Sunlit had hastily kicked out of the way. "And what's this? You didn't tell me you had a whale," he told Fish reproachfully.

"We just got it," Fish explained.

As the boys gathered up whale pieces and sat on the rug to assemble them, Sunlit carefully walked around the edge of the room, tidying things up a little. Her pack and cot stood in the corner nearest the ladder, still quite bare. Fish's things had somehow taken up the center of the room. At the far end, water was still bubbling away in a pot on the camp stove.

"Fish, our noodles will be ready soon," Sunlit called, as she went to finish making dinner.

"You're cooking? There?" Chip's ears went up, then flopped back down in dismay. "You can't cook inside! Everybody knows food tastes better when you cook it outside."

"Is that true?" Fish's eyes were round, whale forgotten.

"You can't just cook on the boardwalk," Sunlit protested. "And this isn't barbecue. This is—"

"Oooh, spicy noodle soup," Chip finished for her. His nose twitched as he came over to inspect their little cooking station.

"Sunlit said she'd make mine not spicy," Fish informed his new best friend as he came over too. "And look! There are tofus. I helped pour them in."

"And veggies, too. Nice," Chip said, nudging Fish companionably. Then he looked back up at Sunlit, eyebrows scrunched as he came to another conclusion. "You don't really like being outside, do you?"

Sunlit balked. "I—well, I don't *not* like it, but—"

"The sun burns her really bad," Fish said helpfully.

"Ohhhhh," said Chip, once more. "Gosh, and I went and told you your fashion wasn't right for the beach. I'm sorry, Professor."

The apology was so simple and so earnest that it rendered

Sunlit speechless at first. After a moment, she managed, "It's alright, Chip. It's not like I—I didn't expect you to know."

"It's good to apologize," Fish said proudly.

Chip rubbed Fish's head, making the little boy laugh.

Watching, Sunlit smiled and decided on a whim to go one step further. "I don't worry as much in the evenings, in the shade. We could eat outside if you want to. Do you—would you want to join us, Chip? There should be enough."

Chip beamed. "I *never* turn down food."

* * *

Sunlit and Fish sat on the side door stoop, while Chip sat cross-legged on the boardwalk facing them. Three servings of soup slowly disappeared as they talked about the beach, the pier, and Fish's favorite topic, the types of animals they had in the Sanctuary so far. He was midway through telling Chip all about Joy's infected tail, for the second time, when Sunlit noticed Officer Ebb walking their way.

At first, her heart plummeted. Were they doing something wrong? Was it against the rules to eat on the boardwalk? To sit in doorways?

But as Officer Ebb solemnly greeted the party and asked her to step aside with him, she got the feeling it might be something even worse.

Sunlit left the pot, which she'd been eating out of since they didn't have three bowls, on the floor of the shop behind her. She picked her way over Chip, who was already entertaining a curious Fish. For that, at least, Sunlit was deeply grateful. She joined Officer Ebb at the edge of the boardwalk nearest the beach, several paces away.

"We have a report from our initial searches," Ebb told her quietly.

"Do we? You?" Sunlit tugged her sleeves down, and wrapped her arms around her body. The shadows didn't quite reach them, but at least Fish and Chip couldn't hear.

"We've conducted exhaustive physical and magical searches into Fish's circumstances," Officer Ebb went on professionally. "For all we can find, it's as though he washed up ashore by himself. He might as well be a part of the ocean, for all anyone can tell. The Witch says there's no trace of any living relative, not within miles. If there was, we could—"

But here, Sunlit's brain caught up with the situation. She'd been surprised at first that they were discussing *Fish*, not herself or the pier; and then she'd been hopeful; and now she was devastated for the child. "No living relatives? No one else survived?"

Officer Ebb hesitated, eyeing her, then softened a little. "It might not be a matter of having survived," he said more gently. "I've had teams out there day and night, and we've found nothing. No new debris from a wreck, no sunken ship. No bodies."

"You're saying maybe there wasn't anyone else to begin with?" Sunlit glanced back to Fish, who was still sitting in the Sanctuary doorway, laughing at something Chip had said. Ige, still in his lifeguard swimsuit, had joined them.

How could it be possible that Fish had no one else?

"Nothing we can find, and that makes me think *nothing* is the right answer," said Ebb, grim. "The Witch says this happens sometimes with victims of curses."

"You think Fish is—*cursed?*" Sunlit had to remind herself to lower her voice.

"That's just one possibility," said the police officer. "We don't know for sure. But either way, it's unfortunate that the kid seems to have no one to look after him. It hardly seems like a blessing, now, does it?"

He has me, Sunlit might have said. It was lurking somewhere in her chest. But she knew what Officer Ebb meant, and she tried to focus on that.

"Is there a—a way to know?" Sunlit faltered halfway through the question; she wasn't sure if she wanted to hear the answer.

Officer Ebb sighed. "I asked the same thing, myself. Turns out, there's all kinds of curses out there, and some don't look the way you expect them to. Depends if it was some kind of retribution, or punishment, or maybe something to do with his ancestors even. It's all very vague and dramatic. So effectively, the answer is, no. Not unless you want to run a bunch of magical tests on him."

"Me? I'm not his official guardian," Sunlit protested. Looking after Fish was one thing, but making such decisions about him and his future was quite another, as far as she was concerned.

"The town council's meeting about it tonight," Ebb said.

Sunlit gaped. "*What?* You—you can't—you can't just tell me I'm—you can't just tell *him* he's—"

"I know," Officer Ebb interrupted, though again his manner was gentle. He lifted his hat with one hand, running his other hand through his gray hair. "I know. We can't tell you you're his guardian now, and we can't subject the poor kid to a bunch of tests. We have to wait and see how things unfold."

Sunlit shifted, looking over her shoulder again. Ige stood beside the doorway with his hands on his hips, glaring at Chip, who was looking back up at him with his ears perked up. Fish, between the two, had his hands clasped as he watched with interest.

"They look so cute," Sunlit said, despite herself. "I don't understand it. All this talk of curses makes no sense to me. But it is—this is awful. I have *no* experience with kids. And Fish needs someone qualified to look after him!"

"You're doing just fine," Officer Ebb said, his voice sympathetic as he replaced his hat. "The town will step in, and *usually*, the council does manage to do what's right. Everyone knows what's at stake here, Miss Haven. We'll make sure it ends up alright."

Memories of Clementina's ire on the boardwalk were not exactly reassuring. *She* certainly would believe Fish was cursed. But even if he was—what then? Sunlit shook her head. It was too much to try to think through. Her thoughts were going in all different directions. She had to remind herself to breathe.

"They're deciding tonight? And you'll tell me tomorrow?" Sunlit asked uncertainly.

"I'll stop by in the morning," the officer promised. "And—Miss Haven? I'd appreciate it if you didn't tell anyone I said the town council is *usually* right."

Sunlit frowned as she turned to him. It was almost on her tongue to say *is that what really matters here?* But when she met his eyes, he gave her a wry smile. He knew it wasn't that important. But he also seemed to have faith in the community.

With a sigh, Sunlit nodded to him and watched him walk away. After taking a moment to gather herself, she walked back over to Ige, Chip, and Fish. In the silvery twilight, the three looked like no troubles or woes could reach them.

But troubles *would* come. Of that, Sunlit was certain. Her own life had been one of constant vigilance: not only against the sun, but later against any misfortune befalling her patients, or any poor health befalling her grandparents—as, inevitably, it did. There wasn't any way to stop it. So she needed to be prepared.

But how could she prepare for something when she had no idea where it might strike next?

11

A Tender Heart

> *Of all magical ailments, curses are the most unpredictable. Their specific conditions and requirements are unknowable to any except the caster. It is often not possible or downright dangerous for a carer to spend the time testing the curse to try to determine its limits. Instead, a cursed animal should be kept away from all others and encouraged to live out its life as best it can.*
>
> —*from* Standard Practices for a Safe & Sanitary Animal Medic

"Who wants dessert?"

Sunlit hadn't *meant* to say it. She usually forgot about dessert, herself. But the moment she saw Fish's smile up close, the thought just came to her.

"It's Ige's treat," said Chip, promptly, as he stood. "He was just saying he owes you for taking in all the wayward souls from the lifeguard hut."

"I was *not* saying that and it is *not* a *hut*," Ige hissed back.

"Is it true the salamander is named after him?" Chip asked Sunlit, eyes alight with mischief.

"I—I didn't ask," Sunlit admitted, distracted.

"Can we get the sparkling ice cream you talked about?" Fish asked Ige, innocent of whatever drama he was stepping into.

Sunlit wasn't sure what to make of the drama either, but she decided to ignore it. Especially when Ige sighed and said, "Fine. I'll take you there now."

"Just let me close up the Sanctuary," Sunlit put in. She didn't want to pass up on sparkling ice cream—whatever that was— but she did want to make sure Joy was safe.

The otter was, naturally, asleep on the shop floor. But her breathing was more even now, and she stirred in dreams. Sunlit smiled. At least *that* part of her mission in Seaside was going to plan. Based on her experience with other large mammals, she guessed that Joy would be on her feet in a day or two.

The other animals were snug in their tanks, too—aside from one unruly parrot.

"*Sherbet!*" Biscuit swooped outside, landing on her shoulder. The nickname made Sunlit's chest tighten, especially after her conversation with Officer Ebb. But she reminded herself to focus on what was in front of her. Sunlit closed the door gently and locked it, then caught up with the three boys, who were already walking slowly down the boardwalk.

If she'd worried that they would ask her what Officer Ebb wanted, she needn't have bothered. They were, once more, deep in their own world.

"Octopuses love ice creams," Fish was saying. He walked in between the two adults, holding their hands.

Sunlit couldn't help but smile. She wondered how he'd convinced Ige.

"Good thing octopuses ate all their noodles, too," Chip said.

"I'm surprised you didn't want seafood," Ige said to Fish. "Make the sailor work for his freeloading dinner."

It was clear to Sunlit that Ige meant Chip, but Fish neglected this part of the comment. "Seafood is slimy," he said.

"You hear that?" Ige's glance at Chip was amused.

"You just have to try the right kind," Chip said, swinging Fish's hand and ignoring Ige. "Pa will make you some, and you'll see. We'll bring it over tomorrow."

"Where's Sunlit?" Fish asked, distracted.

"I'm here," she called, joining them. Biscuit, still riding on her shoulder, announced his presence with a rusty squawk. Rather than admit how long she'd been watching their conversation without joining in, Sunlit asked Ige, "Where are we going? What's 'sparkling ice cream'?"

"You'll see," Ige said. But underneath his stern demeanor, he seemed to smile just a little bit.

They passed Beachy Bakes, closed for the evening, and a number of gift and games stalls where Sunlit tried determinedly to avoid eye contact with the merchants. The night was balmy, and plenty of families still sat on their picnic blankets and towels out on the beach. Couples strode up and down along the waves. The lights of the boardwalk were plentiful and colorful, perfectly made to entertain. It wasn't a university town, but that didn't mean it wasn't effective. *They know what they are doing in Seaside,* Sunlit assured herself. *They know what they are doing . . .*

The four of them had nearly made it to the end of the boardwalk, Fish swinging between Ige and Chip, before they stopped. Without saying anything, Ige steered them toward the beach side, where at the edge of the planks a little wheeled cart was set up. Under a sparkling purple umbrella, a coastal elf in a striped dress beamed at them. The crackling sprays of light danced down over her little purple hat, highlighting her sandy skin and teal eyes. The effect of the spell was so striking that Sunlit worried at first that the entire cart, from fabric umbrella to the purple striped tablecloth that hung down over the cart's wheels, was a fire hazard. But it was, after all, only magic: a charm which the elf conjured with a wave of her hand, using motion to change the bright yellow sparkles to green to blue as Fish watched with eyes nearly popping out of his head.

"Whoa," he said. "Does the ice cream do that too?"

"It does," the elf assured him. "Only a little smaller."

"Four of the original, please, Cherry," said Ige. He held out exact change. Clearly, he was accustomed to doing business with the ice cream stand—perhaps for the sake of his young lifeguard trainees? Sunlit warmed to him a little more.

"You got it." Cherry winked down at Fish. "I'll make yours extra special. Want to see how I do it?"

"Yes please!" Fish crowded the stall. Sunlit opened her mouth to tell him to keep his distance, but Cherry was already showing him where she kept an icebox hidden beneath the tablecloth.

"It's alright, Professor," Chip said, turning to catch the worried look in her eye. "Ige wouldn't support anything dangerous on the beach."

"I would not," Ige agreed, as though agreeing pained him. "The sparkle charm is merely an illusion. Cherry's grandmother was a fairy, and passed down to her this skill."

"It's about all I can do," Cherry added, smiling at Sunlit as she scooped ice cream into a cone. "But it comes in useful, I guess. What do you think?" she asked Fish.

"Can I hold that one while you make the others?" Fish asked.

"You'll be a professional ice cream seller in no time, Fish," Chip observed.

Sunlit felt a twinge. What *would* Fish do with himself? Of course, he was awfully young, too young to be thinking of such things. But still, she couldn't help but—

"Reality to Haven," Chip said, nudging her and interrupting her train of thought. Ige was holding an ice cream cone out to her. Above the creamy vanilla dessert, a little wooden stick with a gold star on top emitted sparkles just like the ones on Cherry's umbrella.

It hardly seemed like *reality*. Not because of the magic—that was common enough—but because of the sudden realization that she was halfway across Beyond from home, worrying about a four year old she'd never asked to be responsible for, about to eat ice cream of all things, in the company of strangers.

"*Sherbet!*" Biscuit squawked again, right next to her ear.

"It's going to melt," Ige warned her.

Sunlit glanced down. Fish was already halfway through his. He held the tiny sparkling wand in one hand like a scepter. Ice cream was all over his face.

"Sorry," she said, taking her cone from Ige. She could feel Biscuit shift on her shoulder as he eyed the sparkling novelty. "It's really nice of you. This evening has just been . . . well, the past few days have all been a little surreal."

"Let's sit over here while we eat," Chip said, quite reasonably. It was doubtful that Fish would be able to eat, sparkle, and walk at the same time. But Sunlit soon found that she hadn't gotten off as easily as she might have thought. Once they were all sitting in a row at the edge of the boardwalk, feet dangling above the sand, Chip went on. "I get that. It's probably been pretty weird to come to town and have us all ask you to do stuff all the time nonstop."

"Oh, I don't mind the doing stuff," Sunlit assured him. He sat on one end, and then Fish, and then herself, Biscuit, and Ige. In looking over to answer Chip, she absently wiped some ice cream from one of Fish's small ears.

"Some of us do have a notion of civic duty," Ige said nobly from his end.

"Ha!" Chip positively chortled over his ice cream, his white tail waving behind him. "Professor, has Ige told you about his less-than-civic past yet?"

"There is no need," growled Ige.

"Oh, come on, I love this story," Chip insisted. "See, a year or two back, when Taiwo and Rei were getting married, it turned out that—"

"One more word and I'll lock you up for disturbing the peace," Ige interrupted.

Chip paused, the sparkler on his ice cream cone illuminating a mischievous glint in his eye. "You can't do that. You're not the police!"

"*Not the police,*" Biscuit squawked, hopping onto a nearby rail.

"Sunlit, look! He really does follow you," said Fish. Apparently, he'd been too wrapped up in excitement to notice the parrot earlier.

"Biz is a very smart bird," Sunlit said absently. "So, um, Chip and Ige, you two know each other pretty well?"

It was a point she'd been wondering about for a while. Especially because of Ige's behavior. He hadn't exactly been *nice* to her—aside from the ice cream—but he also had never claimed extraordinary powers or threatened to fine her, either. That seemed to be behavior he reserved for Chip.

"Not really until after Taiwo's wedding," Chip said. "Though I've lived here all my life. Ige, despite what he'd like you to think, is still a newcomer—"

"I told you, *enough*," Ige insisted.

"Is it bad to be a newcommor?" Fish asked, licking ice cream from his fingers.

"No," said Sunlit, somewhat dubiously. "That's kind of what we both are, Fish. It means someone who only just got here."

"I got here days ago," said Fish. "In the storm!"

"I know it feels like a long time," Sunlit told him, smiling despite herself, "but I think Chip is talking about a lot longer than that."

"Me and my family have been here *forever*, kid," Chip said, rubbing Fish's head. "But don't worry. We'll let you stick around."

"Octopuses have stickers on their arms," Fish declared happily.

Suckers, Sunlit was about to say. She knew it didn't matter, but she'd been a university tutor too long to let the point slide. Before she could open her mouth, however, she found Ige leaning over her shoulder like a storm cloud.

"You should be more careful what you say," he told Chip, his voice suddenly angry.

"You should be more careful what you do," Chip retorted. Unlike Sunlit, he clearly was not intimidated in the least. "Get off the Professor. You're being a boor."

Ige snapped back into place immediately. "Sorry," he mumbled to Sunlit, though it was clear he was still upset about something.

"A little sensitivity wouldn't hurt, you know," Chip added.

"Um," said Sunlit, caught in the middle with Fish, and longing for the safety of peace. "I want to rinse my hands off. Fish, do you want to come?"

"My sparkler's still going," Fish protested. Sure enough, though everyone else's sparkler had dimmed as the spell ran out, Fish's was going strong in rainbow colors. *Extra special, indeed,* Sunlit thought desperately.

"I'll stay here with him," Chip offered. "You can take Ige instead."

Sunlit glanced to her side to see that Ige, too, had finished his cone. Though he glowered, he did not protest. She didn't see a way out of it.

"Good luck," Chip added as they hopped down onto the sand.

"Good luck!" Fish echoed more cheerfully.

"*Luck, luck,*" squawked Biscuit in the background.

Sunlit and Ige made their way toward the dark waves, leaving the bright boardwalk behind. Ige walked stiffly over the sand. Sunlit would have been happy to make the trek in awkward silence, but once they were out of earshot—even certain fluffy white ears—and about halfway to the water, Ige burst.

"*Luck!*" he said, disgusted. "*He's* the one who goes around making promises he can't keep."

"About Fish staying?" Sunlit ventured. Slowly, she started to make sense of the awkwardness she'd been hoping to escape.

Ige frowned out over the ocean, confirming her suspicions. "It's irresponsible."

"I guess you—I guess you heard the news, then," Sunlit concluded. She watched the sand as they closed in on the waves. "Taiwo told you?"

"I do have connections to town other than Taiwo," Ige snapped.

"Sorry. I just figured . . ."

As Sunlit's voice trailed off, Ige sighed heavily. "Or maybe, I don't. Actually it *was* Taiwo who told me. I went over to the Sanctuary to see if you knew, but Ebb was already there."

"You were coming to tell us?" Sunlit wasn't sure what to do with this information.

"What are you going to do?" Ige asked.

They came to a stop, the farthest reaches of the foamy waves reaching their toes. Like Ige, Sunlit looked out over the ocean. The sky was cloudless, and stars twinkled back at her like the sparkles on Cherry's ice cream cones.

"I don't know," she admitted very quietly. "Officer Ebb said he'd know more in the morning. He said he'd come by and let me know . . ."

"That's good, then." Ige kicked at the water, arms crossed. "Chip is too tenderhearted. That's his problem. We must be practical."

"Yeah," Sunlit agreed. Normally she clung to practicality. But now, hearing the gloom in Ige's voice, she wasn't so sure about it. "Ige, if you wanted to hear the news too, if Taiwo doesn't tell you first, you could . . . you could stop by the Sanctuary tomorrow. If you're worried, too? You did find him, after all."

Ige swallowed before he spoke. He kept his arms crossed. "You aren't worried I'll show up with more animals in tow?"

Despite herself, Sunlit laughed. "Fish would probably love it if you did."

12

A Cloudy Dawn

The Great Spring Flood is a perfect example of what made early Seaside thrive. History has shown conclusively that the flood, the greatest flood in Seaside's history—so high that the water topped the bar at the town's tavern—was brought on by misguided weather charms, which backfired. Rather than conduct excessive and unproductive trials to punish the magic-users, the town of Seaside came together to save water-logged provisions and relocate those who lived along the coast.

    —*from* A Guide to Seaside (for the Discerning Tourist)

After a restless night, Sunlit was up too early. She'd tried looking up anything about curses or magic gone awry in her books, but none of it helped her relax. She almost wanted to go back to Rachel's book store to ask for more specific magic reference tomes . . . Instead, she decided to work.

She left Fish snoring in his cot beside the ocean floor rug and made her way down to the shop floor. Using bycatch from the sailors, she prepared food for the animals in the tanks, but hesitated to give it to them. She knew Fish would be sad he missed the event, and after all, the sun was only barely up. No one needed to be fed just yet.

No one except herself, maybe. Her stomach growled loudly. At the noise, Joy shifted and lifted her head, her nose twitching.

"Who's there?" the giant otter asked.

Sunlit came out from behind the counter, smiling. Joy's voice sounded clearer than it had in days. "Sorry to wake you. It's just me. I couldn't sleep, so I've been trying to get some chores done."

Joy stretched, unfurling from her corner spot and reaching her front paws out across the shop. "I used to like getting up early, you know. I can't think what's come over me."

"A near concussion, a forced fast, an infection and a fever, a ruptured tail and a bunch of bruises, that's what came over you," Sunlit said, walking closer to examine her patient in the half-light from the windows.

"When you put it that way," said Joy, "it sounds awful. I assure you it really hasn't been that bad."

Sunlit looked steadily at the otter's large face. Seeing that her eyes were clear and her whiskers straight, Sunlit decided that she must be recovered enough to joke around a little. In response, she smiled. "Well, I'm glad you think that. But that's probably because you've been asleep most of the time."

"But not all the time," Joy insisted. "Where's that little human? Wasn't there one here?"

"There is," Sunlit answered. "He's upstairs, asleep."

"Is that why we are being quiet in the dark?" Joy asked, lowering her voice to a whisper.

"Yes," Sunlit said, amused. "Do you mind if I take a look at your injuries?"

"Be my guest, if you can see them," was the otter's reply. "I can see underwater, but I don't like all this shadow business."

Sunlit retrieved her portable torch from the sales counter to assist. She didn't have good vision in the dark, either, and she didn't want to shock the creatures in their tanks with the bright shop lights just yet. As she knelt beside Joy and started checking one paw at a time, she was reminded of Joy's original situation. "It must have been terrible for you under that boat. Wasn't it very dark, then, too?"

"Just awful," Joy agreed. "But, you know, a little cozy, too."

"With your tail literally bleeding?" Sunlit asked, scandalized.

"I didn't notice that part so much," Joy said thoughtfully. "What is it they say? When you get in a scrape, instinct takes over, and all that."

"That was more than a scrape," Sunlit insisted as she moved down to check the bandaging on Joy's tail.

"Still though, it led to this, which I must say is not so bad," said Joy, stretching her front paws again. "I smell fresh fish for breakfast. Do you *always* put things in the worst light, Miss Sunlit?"

"Just Sunlit or Haven is fine," Sunlit said automatically. She sat back on her heels, struck by Joy's accusation. "I, um, hadn't thought about it that way. Sorry if I upset you. It's just, usually my patients don't talk. Not in the usual sense."

"That explains your lack of bedside manner, then," Joy said kindly. "It's quite alright. Maybe you don't know much yet about joyfulness, but I know you mean well."

"You do?" Sunlit asked, curious.

"I can feel it," Joy assured her. "Is it breakfast time yet?"

I can feel it sounded just like something Sunlit had told her professor, time and time again, about a mysteriously injured patient. But she still got no *feelings* about Joy's injuries. *Perhaps, she was smart enough to realize, because Joy could just tell me about them.*

But that doesn't explain the snail, fish, and others. And she doesn't seem to actually like *talking about her injuries anyway,* Sunlit mused. She considered changing Joy's bandages right away, but decided ultimately to let the poor otter eat her breakfast first. Fortunately, they did have a stash of fish in the icebox under the counter.

"I'm impressed you could smell them," Sunlit admitted, as she pulled them out and opened the container Chip had loaned them.

"Hopeful sensing," Joy said, licking her lips. "I am so hungry, I could eat a whale!"

"I'm a whale!" Fish's voice drew their attention to Fish's head, which hung upside down from the hatch to the attic. "Would you eat me, Joy?"

"You're too small of a whale, child," Joy said, much to Sunlit's relief. "I need a very big meal."

"Fish, be careful," Sunlit added. She rushed over to help Fish down, and then together they fed Joy—and the rest of the animals, much to Fish's delight.

Sunlit had just sent Fish back upstairs to dress for their own breakfast when someone knocked at the front door. She had to steel herself to open it.

It was, as she had expected, Officer Ebb. Despite the early hour, he looked exactly as he did at every other time of day:

immaculate blue uniform, steely blue eyes. Sunlit could not stand it. "Is it good news or bad news?" she asked quietly, leaning in the doorway.

"Depends on what you mean," Officer Ebb said, his dry tone a small comfort. "Town council decided last night that, curse or no, he can stay in Seaside."

"Curse?" Joy's curious voice drifted out from inside.

Sunlit didn't answer yet, her back pressed into the door frame.

"That's as long as no dangerous side effects manifest around him, mind you. But assuming that they won't, the town council has decided to open an application period," Officer Ebb went on, "for those wishing to become the child's guardian."

Sunlit licked her lips. "Applications?"

"Unusual, yes, but the town has done this kind of thing once or twice before," Officer Ebb told her. "Trust the process. And if you should like to submit an application yourself, I brought you one to look over."

He handed her an official document, twisted up like an old scroll. Sunlit took it without a word. As he left, and Joy continued chewing fish, and Fish's footsteps sounded above, she got that feeling of being out of reality again . . .

Should I apply or not?

* * *

Fish, naturally, wanted to go back to Beachy Bakes for breakfast. This was complicated somewhat by the fact that Joy wanted to come with them, to "stretch" her legs. Sunlit stuffed the application into the top drawer in the counter, and tried to shove it out of her mind.

The three spilled out the side door. Biscuit soared out, too, escaping while Sunlit patted her pockets for her wallet and keys. The parrot perched on Joy's shoulder. Joy, who was peering over the side of the pier with Fish, didn't seem to notice or mind a bit.

Sunlit was starting to feel like an apprentice in a circus act. When she heard Ige yelling her name, she was almost relieved. Sure, he might want to talk about difficult things and he could be a little off-putting, but he knew a lot about order and discipline . . .

And yet, she realized, his voice as he was calling her sounded unusually frantic.

"Sunlit! Sunlit! Ige's calling!" Fish added, in case she hadn't noticed.

"*Sherbet!*" Biscuit squawked. The parrot, for some reason, continually refused to use Sunlit's name and stuck solely to her grandparents' nickname for her.

"Oh dear," said Joy. "That doesn't look good."

Sunlit was almost afraid to turn around as she finished locking the door.

Ige was standing out on the beach. It was still early, and he was alone—except for a large lump at his feet. Sunlit had a sinking feeling she knew why he hadn't come over to ask about Fish. He had, clearly, found another creature for the Sanctuary.

Maybe Ige is the cursed one, she couldn't help but think, as she raced over.

The tide was high, forcing her to run across soft dry sand. Holding her hat down with one hand, her keys still dangling from the other, she felt very unprepared for this new crisis. However, she did her best.

"You were calling?" she panted as she came up.

"For three minutes," Ige informed her.

The lump at his feet made a loud sound, possibly an attempt at a roar, but it ended in a cough.

"I don't think it likes me," Sunlit said, stumbling back a pace. She'd never had a patient react that way before. Granted, she'd never actually encountered her patients in the wild before . . .

"It's been doing that since dawn," Ige corrected. "That's why I found it. You can go close to it and it doesn't do anything. See?"

"Don't," Sunlit demanded, unable to stop herself, as Ige leaned down.

Ige snapped back up, crossing his arms. "I wasn't going to poke it or anything. Just roll it over. Why do you and Chip think I'm some kind of monster?"

"Habit from dealing with students, sorry," Sunlit said, amending her tone. "It's not that I thought you were going to do anything bad, it's just that, it's really best not to stress an animal out by getting into its space. Even if it won't hurt you."

Ige stared at her, his dark eyes inscrutable. "Well then how are you going to treat it?"

"Right." Sunlit looked down at the creature. *Was* she going to treat it?

Am I going to apply?

Never mind that, she told herself crossly, refocusing. Joy and Fish had caught up and were standing nearby, but there were no other animal doctors on the beach. She *was* going to treat the creature . . . whatever it was.

First things first. Sunlit paced around the animal—and Ige— walking through the waves to get a thorough look. What had seemed like a large lump turned out to have strong tail flippers, submerged in the surf. The bulk of its body was on dry sand.

Front flippers were wedged uselessly under its belly. Its face was largely obscured by a thick, sand-matted ruff of tawny hair.

"It's a lion seal," Sunlit said, squatting near the creature's head to see its face. Her pants legs were wet, but she ignored the sensation. "A real one—sort of a cross between a seal and a lion. We learned about them in classes, but we never had one at the Marine Center before. They don't live in the waters around New West Key."

"Is it sick?" Fish asked. The little boy had snuck up behind her shoulder.

"I think so," Sunlit replied. "Between the sound it made earlier, and the way its eyes are crusted over—see there?"

"Eww," Fish said, delighted. "It has snot coming from its nose!"

"We can't have this on the beach," Ige reminded them, in what could have been a very good impression of Officer Ebb's wry tones.

"I'm sure it doesn't want to *be* on the beach," Sunlit retorted. "But it also won't want to be inside the Sanctuary. And besides, it's far too dirty, and it could get Joy or the other animals sick. And how do you suggest we move it, anyway?"

"The poor thing." Joy, too, had come closer, and was looking over Sunlit's other shoulder. "Obviously we don't want him to stay here, where every tourist can poke and prod him. If you get a raft or a towel of some kind, maybe one of those large thin towels, I could help drag him, Sunlit."

"You mean a sheet or blanket?" Sunlit wrinkled her nose, thinking. "I suppose that *could* work."

"Why can't he move?" asked Fish, who had clearly not had much experience with sickness in his young life. "Did he get hurt by a boat like Joy?"

"No, but he needs medicine and a lot of sleep, like Joy did," Sunlit said absently. Then, the thought struck her. "Ige—there's a boat overturned between the old pier and the breakwater, up near the bait shop. Not the one Joy was under, but a bigger one."

"One problem at a time," Ige insisted.

"It *is* one problem," Sunlit said, standing to look at him. "Or, I think it could be. Is the boat mine? Since I bought the pier?"

"Most likely," said Ige reluctantly. It was clear he was still confused. "You could ask Taiwo if you want to be sure. But waterfront property usually includes the water around the property, which would include the boat. Why?"

"Get some of your lifeguards," Sunlit said. She was getting excited now. "We can turn the boat rightside up—"

"It still won't float any more," Ige warned—

"I don't want it to," she told him. "I want it to sit against the rocks there, in the shallows. It can be a recovery pool for the Sanctuary."

"We're going to have a pool?" asked Fish.

"The sooner we get this fellow there, the better," said Joy.

The lion seal croaked hoarsely, spitting phlegm onto the sand.

"Fine," Ige said. "Give me half a minute."

13

A Marine Solution

> *The lion seal is one of the few creatures whose origins we know for certain. A professor of magic in Argen wished to summon a lion as a familiar. However, while performing the spell, he was distracted at the last minute by his daughter, who wished to visit the aquarium. Sudden thoughts of marine mammals invaded his mind and thus, a hybrid was born. Though the lion seal is in many respects an admirable cross of both lion and seal, it is perhaps too perfect a predator. Since the professor's innocent mistake, lion seals have spread to coasts across Beyond.*
>
> —*from* Traverse's Guide to Marine Vertebrates, Invertebrates, and Magical Outliers

Ige quickly took over the boat operation, leaving Sunlit, Fish, and Joy to deal with the lion seal. Though she was familiar with various illnesses and colds from her time at the Marine Center, Sunlit felt her lack of "feeling" acutely. She wished she could identify precisely what kind of sickness the lion seal had, but it was impossible, given her current equipment and knowledge.

But it might not matter, she told herself hesitantly. *The best thing for pretty much any sickness of this type will be rest, cough medicine, and some of those vitamin tablets . . .* Fortunately, she still had plenty of those. Joy had never taken to them. And the sailors were already accustomed to selling her all their leftover catch, so the lion seal's diet was easily taken care of.

And the best thing to do is focus on the present. Sunlit put her hands on her hips, unconsciously imitating her professor as she tried to regain her confidence. Priority number one was to remove the patient from any current danger—that was what all her books said, and what she herself *knew* from her studies. Seaside's beach might not seem "dangerous," but as she'd pointed out to Ige earlier, it was not a restful and secure place for a sick animal either. Moving the lion seal toward the boat was definitely the first order of business. Sunlit was just debating which of her precious new blankets to run and get— or if she could risk asking Fish to run and grab one—when someone else called to them.

"Ahoy, there!" Arietta's little form made its way to them over the sand, a spring in her step and a large bundle under her arm. "I was wondering where my best new customers were when I looked outside and saw what was going on. Did you find a new friend?" she asked Fish.

"He has snot coming out of his nose," said Fish.

"Hello," Joy added. "You smell very sweet."

"Joy, this is Arietta. Arietta, Joy," Sunlit said. She was touched by Arietta's friendliness, of course, but mildly annoyed at the interruption. They really didn't have much time before families started arriving on the beach.

"Ah, so you are our famous giant otter. A pleasure to meet you," Arietta said, beaming. "It'll be my baked goods you're smelling. I don't know if they're any good to otters, but I brought some for you and Fish, dear," she added, to Sunlit.

At the thought, Sunlit's stomach rumbled again. "Thank you, Arietta. I'll pay you later, I promise."

"Don't be silly," said Arietta contentedly. "This is my donation to the beach rescue effort. We old citizens like to pitch in, you know. I also brought this, in case you need it."

There was a sound of unfurling. It distracted Sunlit, who had been staring moodily at the lion seal, trying to plan her next steps. But now, she looked up to see that the majority of the bundle Arietta had brought was a large, wax-treated gingham tablecloth.

"I used to have a whole set of them," Arietta explained. "For the shop. But last year, I felt it was time for a change and got new ones from Coral's tailor. I certainly won't be needing this one any more. Do you think you could use it, dear?"

"Actually, we really could," said Sunlit, amazed. "If you don't mind? Um—the lion seal really is very sick. You might not want it back afterward . . ."

"Dear heart, I *know* I don't want it back afterward," Arietta assured her with a smile. "It's yours to use as you wish. Now, what else can I do?"

For a problem which had momentarily baffled Sunlit in the beginning, it took no time at all to solve. They stretched out the tablecloth beside the lion seal and Sunlit carefully rolled the creature onto it. They had fabric to spare—Sunlit couldn't imagine the size of the table Arietta had been using, but she didn't bother asking. The extra room made her more comfortable letting the others help. She took one front corner, and Joy bit down on the other; and Fish and Arietta took up the back corners, suitably matched as train-carriers. While Sunlit and Joy did the heavy dragging, Fish and Arietta helped steer and keep the lion seal in place.

By the time they'd neared the end of the beach, Ige and his crew had successfully turned over the wreck behind the bait shop. They'd even secured it in place with old ropes and some salvaged planks, and Sunlit knew she could trust Ige's declaration that it was "as safe as it's going to get." The difficulty, it turned out, was getting the lion seal *to* it.

The old pier was between them and the boat. The columns supporting the pier were slightly too narrow for the lion seal dragging-team, however, and the hull of the boat was more level with the pier's surface than the beach. Taking the lion seal up onto the boardwalk and then down into the boat from there seemed the best bet. Joy did offer to swim him around instead, but both Ige and Sunlit opposed this—Ige on the basis that going under the old pier was dangerous, and Sunlit because saltwater and wounds made unpleasant company, bandages or no.

With Ige's help, though, going up the beach and making the slight lift up to the boardwalk from the sand was not as bad as Sunlit had feared. Fish and Arietta helped clear the way for them to walk down the pier a few steps, in order to draw even with the boat. As they did, Sunlit paused to assess her new "recovery pool."

The boat was, indeed, lodged firmly between the pier and the breakwater. Its hull was largely intact, but a few holes at the bottom were steadily letting the ocean in. Though the prow, which sat above the high tide line, was dry, water lapped at the bottom of the boat beginning at mid-ship. The boat's stern was nearly underwater, with just a foot or so of weather-beaten wood keeping out the waves. The old steering platform made a natural, shallow step in what was otherwise a pool big enough that Fish would have to tread water.

Not that Fish was allowed, of course. The old wood could hardly have been child-safe, and truthfully the entire vessel would have been rejected out of hand as an animal refuge, back at the Marine Center. But needs must, as Sunlit reminded herself. It could use a bit of sanding, refinishing, and a little spellwork perhaps, but for now, it was a very good resting place for a sick lion seal.

"This is perfect," she told Ige, satisfied. "Let's try lowering him gently, over by the stern."

* * *

By the time Sunlit had finished cleaning up the lion seal and giving him a vial of cough syrup from her traveling medical kit, the sun was high over the beach. The glare off the water made her nervous, something she hadn't noticed while she was focused on her work, but which hit her full force as soon as she was done.

She found Ige sitting in the Sanctuary's side door, as though the place was his. But since he offered her the breakfast she'd forgotten earlier, she didn't protest. She took the egg sandwich and dropped into the shade next to him.

"Joy's inside asleep," he said, before she could ask. "Arietta took Fish for a little while."

"At the bakery?" Sunlit hesitated. Fish was an excellent

helper, but unlikely to be proficient in food safety; and how well did she really know Arietta, anyway?

"You can literally see it from here," Ige reminded her. "She said she was going to have Fish color new signs for her."

"Well, he might like that," Sunlit admitted, relaxing slightly. "I don't have any coloring things here."

I don't have any kid things, she thought. *What exactly do I think I am doing?* The rolled-up application floated through her mind again, and she swatted it away.

"Yes," said Ige, noncommittally. Sunlit looked up, worried for half a second that he'd answered her thoughts rather than her words, somehow. But his face was impassive. "Ebb came by to check up on reports about the lion seal situation. He filled me in."

The Sanctuary was becoming quite the hub of town life, but Sunlit didn't notice that part at first. She picked at her sandwich, uncertain. "What do you think?"

"What can I think?" Ige shrugged. "It's the best idea anyone could come up with. I just hope someone applies. Before something else goes wrong."

"What do you mean?" Sunlit tucked her boots further into the shadow, closer to herself. "You don't think anyone will?"

Ige looked out over the beach, his gaze keen and practiced, looking for trouble. "The Witch isn't what I'd call discreet. Rumors have gotten around."

"What? How could they?" Sunlit had never felt so irrationally angry at someone she'd never met before.

"It doesn't help that he showed up right after a storm," Ige pointed out. "And he goes around saying he did it and that he's a sea monster all the time. People believe him."

"I get that it could be unsettling," Sunlit admitted. She

wracked her brain—today, Fish was saying he was a whale; surely he couldn't scare Arietta's customers too much with that? It was better than shark or kraken. "But does anyone really know what he means? It could be his imagination."

"It's not just his imagination when he makes waves appear out of nowhere," Ige said, his voice still bland. "He obviously has magical heritage of some kind, and not just sleight-of-hand stuff like Cherry's. He could be a shapeshifter. He could be an actual sea creature that got caught up in some spell. I've even heard people say that the old exiled witch down the shore created him as a magical familiar to spy on the town."

"That's ridiculous," Sunlit protested, rather hotly for someone who knew very little about magic.

Ige looked at her, finally. "You hear a lot of things, out on the beach. I'm not saying I believe it."

"I hope no one does," Sunlit declared. Then, more desperately, "Ige—I really hope no one does. They can't. He needs to have a home."

"People seem okay with him being here at the Sanctuary, for the most part," Ige returned. "They think you can keep him contained, since you're a university expert."

This, in Sunlit's opinion, was *also* ridiculous, but she bit her tongue.

"Anyway," Ige said, shifting back toward the beach, "eat your sandwich. And maybe think about lunch. I have to leave soon for my shift."

"You haven't been at work this whole time?" Sunlit asked, around a mouthful of her breakfast. She'd taken Ige's advice, only to regret it when he brought up a questionable point.

"No. I was just out for—it doesn't matter. I work the afternoon today," he said.

"Is—is Chip right about you?" Sunlit smiled hesitantly, glad for the distraction. "Are you one of those people who's always at work?"

"You're one to talk," said Ige, gruffly. And then, too casually, "What else does he say about me?"

"Who, Chip?" Sunlit took another bite, thinking about this. "Nothing you wouldn't expect."

Ige bristled. "What's that supposed to mean?"

"I mean, you've got to know you pick fights with him," Sunlit protested.

"Oh, that." Ige settled, though he still grimaced. "If only he wasn't so happy-go-lucky."

"Yeah," said Sunlit, thinking absently of Joy. "I hear you. But sometimes, I do wonder if they aren't right."

14

A Fluffy Confirmation

Arietta sent Fish back to the Sanctuary with two enormous sandwiches as his "wages" for the morning. While they sat and ate—again, in Sunlit's case—Fish told her happily about his re-branding of Beachy Bakes.

"I used orange," he explained, "because orange is whales' favorite color."

"How many whales did you survey to know that?" Sunlit asked, her mind far away.

Fish picked an old piece of spinach off of his sandwich. "Survy?"

"Survey," she repeated, refocusing on him with a smile. They'd retreated inside the bait shop, sitting on camp chairs behind the sales counter. Nevertheless, Biscuit was on hand to pick up discarded vegetable matter. "It means how many whales did you ask first. You have to eat your whole sandwich, you know."

"I know. I'm hungry. Whales eat lots. I asked a lot of whales first to know that," Fish said, taking a huge bite that sent more pieces of spinach and pickle rounds to the floor.

"Really? Where'd you meet all those whales?" Sunlit asked, nudging Biscuit away from the pickle with her boot.

"We have a whale boardwalk," Fish informed her. "It's really big, and everything sparkles!"

"Hmm." Sunlit was struck by a thought. Her level of belief in a whale boardwalk was very low, but she had learned how effective it was to get Fish to talk by focusing on marine fantasies. Could she use this to her advantage to learn more about him? "Is the whale boardwalk around here?"

"Whales can go really far to get to a boardwalk," Fish said. *Most likely true, but not useful,* thought Sunlit. While she was musing, Fish went on, "Did you learn about survies as a Professor?"

"Surveys," Sunlit corrected offhandedly. "I learned about them at university, yes. We did lots of surveys to learn about animal health."

"What if you surveyed the lion seal?" Fish asked, squishing his sandwich to better fit into his unfortunately *not* whale-sized mouth.

"I did examine him," Sunlit said. Somehow, her sandwich was already gone. Surveying the lion seal had been more work than she'd realized. "Usually we only say 'survey' if there are a bunch of animals involved. Usually the same kind of animal, too."

"Are people animals?"

"Yep." She found she was smiling affectionately at him now. Talking to Fish was a little like being a university tutor again—although, quite frankly, Fish asked more interesting questions than most of her fellow students had. "Pretty much everyone's an animal. Unless you're made of magic."

"*I'm* not made of magic," Fish reminded her. "I'm made of whale."

"As long as you're not made of rubber, like your whale upstairs," Sunlit conceded. Another new thought occurred to her. She'd assumed that he'd read the labels on his puzzle—but that might be an entirely false assumption. He might have simply liked the picture. And they didn't have many labels in the Sanctuary yet, so they hadn't talked much about words before. "Fish, when you were coloring Arietta's signs, could you read the letters? Do you know what they said?"

"What's a letters?" Fish asked, eating a slice of cheese off his sandwich.

Sunlit pursed her lips. He reminded her very much of Joy referring to both tablecloths and sheets as "towels." There wasn't much need for linens or alphabets in the ocean.

But now that's assuming he's literally from the ocean, she warned herself.

"Letters are the symbols that are on signs," she said. "I look at the letters and I can see that the name on the sign is 'Beachy Bakes.' Or that this bottle—" she reached for one out of the box that the lifeguards had donated the day before—"has sunscreen potion in it."

"What if you had sunscreen potion, but *really strong?*" Fish asked, distracted.

Sunlit sighed. Obviously Fish had no use for letters, since he had adults to ask what things were!

"Or what if you put on *all* the sunscreen potion bottles?" he added, chewing.

"It doesn't work that way," Sunlit said. "I'd still get burned."

"Maybe you're cursed," Fish suggested cheerfully.

Sunlit froze. "Where did you learn about curses?"

"People at the bakery," he told her. "They said curses are bad and people could get hurt. But Arietta said curses are all in your head and you should be shamed."

"Ashamed, probably." Sunlit's shoulders sagged in relief. Though now she was worried that watching Fish really had caused trouble for the baker. "Did they say anything else?"

Fish shrugged. "They didn't like it when I made a wave."

"Inside?" Sunlit tensed right back up.

"It was outside. Because the plants were thirsty," Fish explained. "Can I be done now?"

"*Done now!*" Biscuit squawked, hopping toward the door. At the sudden noise, Joy—curled up in her corner—shifted and slowly lifted her head.

Sunlit sighed. She had cleanup to do, and she wanted to check on the lion seal again, and fix up the old boat a little more to make it habitable. And now, she added *apologize to Arietta* to the list.

Looking down at the mashed bit of bread leftover from Fish's sandwich, she decided it was indeed time to get back to work. "Sure, Fish, you can be done. Want to help me check on Spick and Spann?"

* * *

Sunlit threw herself into her duties, and it was hours before she focused on something that wasn't a marine animal or Fish. It *was* a familiar call, though.

"Professor!"

Sunlit sat up, her back aching from leaning over the submerged wood of her new boat-shaped recovery pool. While the sick lion seal basked in the prow, she had decided to remove any splinters or debris from the stern. And so, Chip found her sitting in water, soaking her legs and butt, her long sleeves wet up past the elbows.

"That's one way to stay cool, huh?" Chip beamed as he walked out on the pier. "Nice to see you up, Joy! And what are you doing to help, little buddy?"

Like the lion seal, Joy basked in the light—but at a safe distance, on the pier, per Sunlit's request. The last thing the giant otter needed was a persistent cough, especially right after her infection seemed to have cleared up. She nodded politely to Chip and let Fish explain himself.

"I have to guard the bucket," Fish said proudly, from his post beside the boat. It was as near as Sunlit wanted him to get to the lion seal, just in case. She'd told him she needed him to look after the debris she pried up, and Fish had seemed content with the task. "Look! Sunlit let me wear her extra hat. Whales don't like too much sun."

"Don't they?" Chip tugged playfully at the hat in question as he joined them, and winked at Sunlit. "That's probably for the best. I brought you something, and someone for you to meet!"

"Something *more*?" Sunlit stretched her arms behind her back, looking toward the boardwalk to see if she could guess what it was this time. Chip was rapidly proving to be a one-man donation center.

"I promised you I'd bring you proper seafood for dinner," Chip reminded them all. Joy licked her lips as she sat up, casting a large shadow over Fish. To Fish, Chip added, "Sunlit wasn't going to make you work past dinner time, was she?"

"We've been working since lunch," Fish said solemnly. "Except, I did have one nap. And so did Joy."

"Good for you, kid. You're entitled to breaks, both of you," Chip said, chuckling. "Oh, good, here he comes now."

Sunlit glanced back toward the shop again, her broad-brimmed hat casting a long shadow. The sun *was* lower in the sky than she had realized: the day had gotten away from her. That had happened often at the Marine Center, of course, but she did feel badly now about Fish. He had never once complained.

And now, around the corner of the shop, came someone else she wasn't too sure about. One thing stuck out about him, though: he looked very much like Chip.

He had the same wolfish white ears and deeply tanned skin. However, his thick white hair had slightly less luster, and it was much longer, brushed back into a low ponytail. He wore a sailor's cutoff pants and loose striped shirt. At a distance, the biggest difference was the way he moved: slowly, carefully, and a little stooped over.

"Everyone, this is Pa," Chip declared as the stranger closed in. "Pa, this is everyone. Meet the new Marine Sanctuary."

"Is that what it says on our sign?" Fish asked Sunlit.

"We don't have a sign yet," Sunlit told him.

"Pleased to meet you," Joy said, remaining focused on the newcomer—and the promise of dinner. "You smell like tasty rock shrimp."

Sunlit sighed. Sometime, later, maybe she would remember to explain to Joy that it wasn't always appropriate to greet people by telling them that they smelled.

"Ahoy, everyone." Chip's Pa had a wide, easy smile that echoed his son's, and his blue eyes twinkled as he looked down at Sunlit and her repurposed boat. "Heard a lot about you. Nice wreck you have here."

"I'm Sunlit Haven," she said apologetically. "We were just finishing up. This is Fish, and behind him is Joy."

"Pleased to meet you. Might as well call me Pa," was the answer, as the retired sailor nodded at each of them in turn. "Everyone does, seems like."

"We're really grateful to you and your son," Sunlit said, trying not to be awkward as she stood up and became aware once more that seventy percent of her clothing was soaked. It was tough, thick fabrics, nothing cloying, but still not very presentable and tidy.

Pa didn't seem to notice anything wrong, though. He laughed. "Grateful? Woulda thought you'd want to smack him upside the head."

"Wouldn't be the first time," Chip told them all, grinning crookedly. "Pa says I meddle. I say he sounds like Ige."

The entire boardwalk seems to meddle, Sunlit couldn't help but think, as she tried to figure out the most graceful way to join everyone at the pier. Flopping herself up onto the boards from the stern, a few feet below the pier's edge, was what she had done without an audience.

"Without you, we wouldn't have met," Joy told Chip. She sounded much more warm and grateful than Sunlit had.

"What's mettle?" asked Fish.

"Chip, offer your hand to your friend," Pa insisted. "Talk over dinner back at the shop."

"Sorry, Sunlit, I wasn't paying attention." Chip reached his hand down to her and hauled her up, still grinning. "You need some ladders. Pa can make you the perfect rope ones, whatever size you need."

Pa sized up the boat once more with a professional's glance. "Two ladders, one for the side, one for the bait shop door," he decided. "Got the rope back home."

Sunlit stood on the pier, surprised. She had entirely forgotten about the back door of the bait shop. It would now open directly over the boat's prow, and a little rope ladder would be perfect for quick access to patients. She was speechless.

"Come on," Joy said, nudging her along. "Shrimp are waiting!"

"I'm not sure whales like shrimp," said Fish. "I didn't do a survey."

"You won't have to. You're going to like these," Chip assured him. "Don't you worry."

"Food's back this way," Pa said, as everyone began shuffling back toward the Sanctuary.

Sunlit let Joy and Fish go on ahead, then cleared her throat as she leaned in to Chip. "Are you sure your father won't mind? We don't have a lot of utensils or chairs, and all these rumors about Fish—"

"We have the pier, and that's enough," Chip told her firmly. "We'll picnic with you. And as for curses—no one worth their salt is afraid of those."

15

An Uncertain Respite

> *The Seaside Beach Lifeguards honor one of the town's most long standing traditions. In fact, Seaside was the first settlement in Beyond to have official lifeguards, paid for by sales taxes and marina fees collected by the town council. The council of Seaside recognized early on that tourists drowning was no good for business . . .*
> *—from* A Guide to Seaside (for the Discerning Tourist)

When Sunlit took Fish to Beachy Bakes the next morning to apologize, she found she needn't have bothered. Arietta laughed her off, and not only that, she provided Fish with his very own whale-shaped cake pop.

"It's my fault anyway," she assured Sunlit, leaning over the counter on her stool as Fish galloped around the tiny store, making his sugary whale "swim" along the walls. "I'm always forgetting those baskets out front. I'm afraid I never did have much of a green thumb."

Sunlit didn't consider herself green-thumbed, either, but she took plant care as seriously as any other kind of caretaking. A question occurred to her and she blurted it out. "Was it saltwater or freshwater?"

"Pardon, dear?" Arietta blinked.

"The wave that Fish made appear to water the plants. Was it saltwater? That's not good for them, right?"

"I wish it was. Maybe if they weren't so picky, they'd be easier to keep alive," Arietta remarked. She leaned back with her hands tucked in her apron pocket, thinking. "I really can't say what kind of water it was. I didn't think to check. And of course my hands were full with—"

"Of course," Sunlit interrupted hastily. She found she didn't want to hear how mad people had been at Fish. "Oh, well, it was just a thought. I don't know if it means anything either way."

She proceeded to place her order and insisted on paying this time, though it did cut into her reserves. *I should probably just make us breakfast at the shop,* she couldn't help but think. But she hated cooking breakfast, and Fish loved his muffins and his new whale pop so much . . .

And Arietta, of course, was still talking. "One kind of magic's much like another, if you ask me, dear. They're all a bit unpredictable in the early days. I'm a firm believer that everything will turn out just fine. And I'd be happy to have my young assistant back, any time. Isn't that right?"

This last bit was directed at Fish, who beamed. Sunlit hustled him out the door before he volunteered for something that would get them both in even more trouble.

In fact, they had barely left the bakery before Fish had his next work request. Ige met them on the boardwalk and asked if Fish would like to be "junior lifeguard" for a morning. Fish, of course, was overjoyed.

Sunlit, on the other hand, wrinkled her eyebrows under her handy straw hat.

Ige pulled her aside. "I *am* on shift this morning."

"I wasn't thinking that," Sunlit protested, although now she definitely was wondering why Ige was so determined to prove Chip wrong all the time. "I was thinking, is it really a good idea? Arietta said she was glad to have Fish yesterday, but he *did* nearly drown her hanging baskets, and apparently some customers—"

"I don't care," Ige said, cutting her off. "That's part of why I wanted to do it. Let them see that they're wrong."

"Are you sure that *is* what they'll see?" Sunlit asked.

"Just go and do errands or something," Ige insisted. "You've been wanting a break, haven't you?"

"Not exactly," she said at once. *Breaks* weren't usually on her mental schedule. But the thought of just running about town quickly to get some things done did have its appeal. She needed to check the post office: maybe Professor McAlpin had good news about the pier situation. And maybe she could pop in at the bookstore, tell Rachel she'd been reading her books. "But, fine. I'll be back before lunch. Just make sure he doesn't . . ."

Fish was running across the sand, "racing" one of Ige's trainee lifeguards, kicking sand everywhere and leaving a wet trail in his wake.

"Just make sure they're safe," Sunlit said, resignation in her voice. She wasn't even sure which *they* she meant. Early morning beach walkers were already looking on—with interest or with suspicion, they were too far away to tell.

Ige snorted. "Like I'd do anything else."

Admittedly, the town's senior lifeguard *did* seem like the last word in safety, when it came to baby-sitters. Probably more safe than a baker with a shop full of sugar and pipettes, in retrospect. Sunlit gave in to the inevitable at last, and took her leave.

Since Joy was looking after the Sanctuary, she really did have the morning free. The feeling was an alien one, and she immediately filled it with things to do. After checking in at the shop and explaining the situation, she took a bucketful of iron—salvage and debris from the wrecked boat, mostly in the form of chain links and hooks—to the market, where she traded the useful metal for some more food and necessities. Her little travel kit of soap and shampoo was not holding up, especially with two people to look after. Rather than think about the implications of the fact that she now owned a full-size shampoo bar and extra toothpaste tablets, Sunlit moved on to the next errand. She had a little extra money—certainly enough for more stamps. She went to the post office on the edge of town and tried to hide her disappointment that, once again, there was no news for her from New West Key. Instead, she sat down to write a letter. It had become a reflex at this point.

Biscuit, who had opted to follow her, did not seem to think much of this activity.

Outside the post office there was a bench and a little table with an umbrella, a spot which had become familiar to Sunlit in her last-minute letter-writing. But as she sat there and wrote out a report for Professor McAlpin in her notebook, Sunlit had to stop frequently to reprimand Biscuit. He seemed to have decided that her pencil would make a tasty snack.

Dear Professor,

Everything well here. Otter alert and aware now, tail recovering nicely. More patients came to the Center. A saturn snail that will need time to fix a ruptured shell. A pair of alpha fish that just need R&R. A crab and salamander damaged in the same storm that injured Joy. Fortunately, we got some nice tanks from the local thrift shop for a good price. If the University takes over the shop, they'll find it's fairly well set—

"Would you stop?" Sunlit hissed at the parrot, when he'd interrupted one sentence for the third time.

"*Curses!*" Biscuit replied.

"You hush," Sunlit said, far more harshly than she'd meant to.

"Trouble in paradise?" asked a friendly voice.

Sunlit looked up to see Chip standing before her. At first, his presence seemed almost inevitable, and she didn't think to question it. But then she realized it was still morning.

"Shouldn't you be out? Fishing?" she replied, frowning.

"We all take a day off once in a while," Chip said. Casually, he pulled out the chair across from her and flung himself into it. Biscuit immediately hopped over to him, and Chip patted his feathers in a friendly way. "Where's the kid? And Joy?"

"Joy offered to look after the Sanctuary . . ." As she said it, she realized that pre-Seaside Sunlit would *never* have allowed a patient to take charge. It was far too unorthodox—the kind of thing that wouldn't even be mentioned in the pages of her old battered copy of *Standard Practices for a Safe & Sanitary Animal Medic*, that's how unthinkable it was. The thought was discouraging. "And Ige said he wanted Fish to be 'junior lifeguard' for the morning."

"Wow, so he *does* have a heart. Who'd have thought," Chip commented.

"Don't you start. I've had enough of talking to you two about you two," Sunlit said, leaning back in her chair and tugging her hat down.

"I wasn't talking about anything," said Chip, innocently. "Are you alright, Professor? You seem like something's eating you."

"It's just . . ." Sunlit sighed. "I still haven't had any letters. It's been five days."

Chip reached behind himself to a potted snake plant, and pulled off a loose leaf to tease Biscuit with. "You got a hot date back in the Key you're waiting to hear from? Devoted partner? Worried they're going—"

"There's no one," Sunlit interrupted, more for her sanity than anything else. Briefly she thought of cute Rachel at the bookstore, but she pushed the thought away. "I mean, I do have an aunt, but she's traveling. I've never had time for romance. No, I was hoping to have heard from my professor—an *actual* professor. But she's probably been busy at a conference . . . and I missed it."

"*Biz! Biz!*" squawked Biscuit as he hopped back and forth, sparring with Chip's leaf.

"Sure, but they have those things all the time, don't they?" said Chip, more on topic.

"I guess so," said Sunlit, miserably. "It's not like I was going to present a paper or anything, I guess. I hate getting up and talking in front of everyone. But still, I . . ."

Chip let Biscuit snatch away the leaf, and turned to study her more seriously. "I'm guessing you weren't hopping up and down at the chance to volunteer and come all the way out here." His dark eyes were soft and kind.

"No, I wouldn't put it that way at all," Sunlit agreed. "To be honest with you, I really didn't think I was the right choice."

"But you must see now that you were wrong, right?" Chip set his elbows on the table and leaned in, making a disgruntled Biscuit fly down to the ground nearby. "Do you know anyone else who could have set up the Sanctuary *and* looked after Fish?"

"I wasn't planning on doing either of those things," Sunlit protested, not realizing that she wasn't answering Chip's question. "Anyway, what are you doing here? Doesn't your mail get delivered?"

"Sure, they deliver mail, even out here in the sticks." Chip's eyes sparkled. "Can you keep a secret?"

Uncertainly, Sunlit nodded.

"I'll whisper, since I know Biscuit can't keep his beak shut." Chip leaned in a little farther. "Pa and I are going to apply to take care of Fish."

"What?" Sunlit leaned back so fast her chair hit her back before she could think.

"Not trying to steal your thunder, of course." Chip resumed speaking in his normal, easy voice. "We could do a sort of split-custody thing, if you wanted. I just thought, you might get real busy with the Sanctuary, or going to conferences or something. And Pa never throws out anything, so we still have my old kid stuff. Plus, Pa totally took to him yesterday, and—I just thought it might be nice for him to have options."

Sunlit was still reeling. "Really? You really are applying?"

"One hundred percent," Chip confirmed.

Thoughts of her own application, still rolled up and tucked

away, entered her mind and she quickly squashed them. "But—why come out here? Do you need some kind of postage for it?"

Chip chuckled. "They have the applications out for people to take at all the town buildings. I could have gone to town center, but that's where the council meets, and I always manage to run into Taiwo there. No offense to Taiwo or anything, but I knew they'd tell Ige, and I don't want him to know yet."

"Why not?" asked Sunlit, numbly. Despite her attempts at squashing, the thought of her own application still haunted her.

"Because he's a certified ruiner of good ideas," Chip said matter-of-factly. "Plus, he gets weird about me doing stuff. Did I tell you about the time he banned me from the beach? All I was doing was trying to break the town breath-holding record. I probably would have, if he didn't hate fun so much."

Sunlit shook her head slowly, willing her emotions to settle into something rational. "Chip, I think . . ."

"Yes?" Chip smiled at her, his ears perking up.

"Never mind," Sunlit sighed. "I just was going to say, I think it's wonderful you're going to apply. I know Fish would love spending more time with you."

"Thanks, Professor, that's sweet of you. And I promise," said Chip solemnly, "not to challenge him to see how long he can hold his breath. Not for a while, at least."

16

A Colorful Encounter

> *It is essential that a medic be fully rested and in the best form when dealing with animals' lives. Therefore, regular rest and time away from surgery are highly encouraged. No medic should be without at least one good assistant or, at the very least, firm working boundaries.*
>
> —*from* Standard Practices for a Safe & Sanitary Animal Medic

Chip didn't so much *insist* on accompanying Sunlit on the rest of her errands, as much as just *not go away*. He waited patiently while she finished and posted her letter. And then he walked beside her on the road back into town, chatting the whole way about the kinds of strange fish he'd encountered while out on the seas around Seaside. It was, admittedly, very interesting. Sunlit had only seen old woodcut pictures of parachute fish, and she was secretly pleased at how impressed Chip was to hear that she'd once tended a sea dragon.

"It was just a baby," she told him, but nonetheless he was on the tips of his toes with excitement. "Someone brought it into the Center after it wouldn't stop following their boat. It had lost its pod and . . ."

Her voice trailed off as they passed a toy store with brightly colored childrens' books in the window. It was a bright, hot day, and everyone was at the beach: Main Street was relatively empty, even though it was nearing lunch time. Sunlit paused on the sidewalk. She *did* have some leftover money from her trade at the market earlier, but it hardly felt right to buy a book from someone other than Rachel. And yet, this one was perfect; and it would only take a moment . . .

Chip followed her into the store without question. When he saw what he wanted to buy, he nodded.

"He can't read yet," Sunlit said, nervously running her hands over the large cloth-bound picture book embossed with sea animals of all types. "If he's going to stay in town, or anywhere with people, he'd better learn, he'll have to go to school anyway, and—"

"I think it's awesome," Chip said, leaning over her shoulder to thumb through the book, a children's introduction to animals of the deep sea. "Look at all the critters they have!"

"I think he'll like it." Sunlit relaxed, reassured by Chip's approval. "I think I have the right change for it . . ."

While Sunlit moved toward the merchant at the back of the shop, rummaging through her coin purse, Chip moved along with her. "We could stop by Coral's, too, and see if she has any new puzzles."

"That could be a good idea," Sunlit said, thinking of the

multitude of blue whale parts scattered across the attic at the Sanctuary. "Something a little more simple, maybe."

The young man at the toy shop was lovely, and wrapped up the book in brown paper in about two seconds flat. In no time, Chip and Sunlit were on the street again. But the sun was high, and she couldn't help but worry a little.

"I said I'd be back by lunch," she told Chip, "and I still have to get something for everyone to eat."

"Ige's making you run errands for *him* now, too?" Chip asked, avoiding a pair of fighting children and their beleaguered father with expertise.

"No, he didn't ask," Sunlit said. "But I just thought I ought to, since he's been watching Fish."

"He ought to be grateful for the chance to let loose a little," Chip told her, with complete confidence. "Still, if you're set on getting us all lunch, I know a great deli. It'll be my treat—the cheese monger there owes me a favor, anyway. They're really fast there, too, so we definitely have time to go to the consignment shop."

He steered Sunlit down the side street toward Coral's Consignment, and she let him. There didn't seem much point in arguing. And she *had* been curious about the town deli. All this business of favors and gifts was unfamiliar, but—*maybe it's nice*, Sunlit decided. Underneath her sunhat she smiled a little to herself, holding her paper-wrapped book close. New West Key was so busy, so wrapped up in university affairs and giant shipping operations. She'd never really considered what life might be like if it was a little slower, a little more personable.

Her feelings of warmth towards Seaside's residents dimmed a little, however, when they got to the consignment shop.

It started out just fine. Chip pulled her into the puzzle corner, much like Fish had. Coral was at the counter, selling some tourists a pair of paddles. But Sunlit overheard whispers and a quick intake of breath. She could feel the tourists' eyes on her strangely as they skirted toward the exit, and once they were gone, Coral came over.

"I'm sorry, I'm afraid—oh." Coral paused and looked around Chip and Sunlit as though they might be hiding something—or someone. "It's just the two of you?"

"Who else were you expecting?" Chip asked, friendly.

Sunlit had a sinking feeling that she knew.

Coral seemed to read the expression on Sunlit's face, and smoothed her hands down over her slim hips. Her dress today was white and covered in pastel flowers. It was almost cruelly at odds with the hard tones she'd taken at first. "Sorry," she said, a little more genuinely this time. "I'm happy to sell you anything you like, but . . . that's just the thing, see. This is a business."

"Why was there a question about selling us things?" Chip continued with his same friendly voice, but the edge was becoming apparent. His ears were back. "This is, as you point out, a shop."

Sunlit watched Coral, distressed at how quickly the tears rose in her throat.

"It's the rumors," said Coral. "They're not good for business."

"What rumors would those be?" Chip pressed, now with downright frightening pleasantry.

Coral looked between Chip and Sunlit. Sunlit didn't dare open her mouth. She knew she wouldn't be able to speak evenly.

"Maybe it's best you leave," Coral said stiffly.

"That does seem like what you've been hinting at," Chip

agreed. "Looks like it's true. Paying attention to rumors *is* bad for business. Come on, Professor, we can spend our money somewhere else."

Sunlit let Chip take her hand. She didn't look at Coral as they hustled out.

But they didn't go far. Chip stopped on the sidewalk outside the shop and shook himself vigorously, from the tips of his ears all the way down his fluffy tail. "Oof," he said. "I *hate* when people get like that. You okay, Sunlit?"

"Just glad Fish wasn't with us," she whispered hoarsely.

"You and me both. But hey, it doesn't have to be that bad," Chip told her. To her shock, he stepped in and gave her a quick hug. "People can be awful, but it usually passes. You'll see. In a few days, everyone in Seaside will move on to the next big story and forget they were ever afraid of the poor kid."

Chip rocked on the balls of his feet, already ready to move on. But Sunlit was rooted to the spot. She lifted her gaze to meet his eyes for the first time. "Do you really think that? But what if they're right?"

"Who cares if they are?" Chip patted her shoulder. "We can handle whatever happens. Together. Now come on, really. I'm starving, and Ige will give me a hard time if I get you back to the beach late. Besides, I can't wait to see Fish's face when you give him that book. Race you to the deli?"

* * *

Naturally, the moment Sunlit and Chip made it to the beach, Ige and Chip began fighting. Never mind the fact that they'd brought a literal picnic basket (turned out, the deli owner owed Chip a *big* favor) filled with bottled lemonade, herbed bread,

140

cheese, fresh veggies, and several jars of spreads in order to share it with everyone.

"What do you think you're doing now?" Ige asked irritably, as Chip approached the lifeguard station with basket in tow.

"Oh, sorry, is *living* not allowed on the beach these days?" Chip retorted. "The Professor wanted to share her lunch with you, but we can just eat it ourselves at the Sanctuary. Come on, Fish!"

"Hi, Chip!" Fish raced over from where he'd been climbing on the lifeguards' rescue dinghy. "Hi, Sunlit! Guess what I am?"

Whatever magic or true shape he might have was as inscrutable as ever. But now he was also wearing a little orange life vest, riding up over his pale teal skin. *It's teal, now?* Sunlit shook her head. Truthfully, Fish amazed her. But the amazement could so quickly turn to worry, when strangers were determined to single him out.

"*Sunlit* wanted to share her lunch with me?" Ige was saying meanwhile, suspicion in every word. His indigo eyes never left Chip's face.

"I told her you're a bore, but she insisted," Chip said airily. "Looks like she needn't have bothered, anyway, if you're just going to turn it down."

"I haven't turned anything down yet. Let a person make up their own mind!"

Sunlit felt like an unnecessary prop in a schoolhouse play. She was almost relieved when Fish came up and tugged her sleeve. "Can you guess? None of the lifeguards could guess except Ige!"

"Good for him," she said, smiling down at Fish's upturned face. The true miracle, Sunlit thought, was that Ige had convinced Fish to wear a life jacket. "Are you a puffer fish? Some of those are orange, too."

"Close!" Fish beamed. With both small hands, he slapped the front of his life jacket, making a wet squelching sound. "I'm a seal! Seals need lots of blubber to keep them warm!"

"Oh, that's your blubber?" In spite of herself, Sunlit chuckled.

"We're going to the Sanctuary," Chip announced, turning to herd both Sunlit and Fish off the beach. "If you want lunch, you'd better make up your mind fast."

"I want lunch!" Fish declared.

"Of course you do." Chip grinned down at him as they walked. "How many lives did you save today?"

"Bunches," said Fish. "Because I made no storms come, so no one got hurt like Joy. Is Joy going to have lunch too?"

Sunlit winced, looking at the nearest family in their row of beach chairs. Everyone quickly avoided eye contact.

"We got Joy something special," Chip assured Fish. In fact, there was a wrapped parcel of trout at the bottom of the picnic basket, keeping cool. It wasn't quite enough to satisfy a giant otter's appetite, but hopefully it would make a pleasant treat.

Sunlit hugged her arms around herself, letting Chip and Fish carry on the conversation without her. It was hard to shake the looks she'd seen that morning, from the tourists, from Coral . . . She'd thought of Coral as a friend, or at least, a friendly acquaintance. Did Coral now regret selling her those lovely fish tanks? Sunlit couldn't help but wonder.

"I take it you had a successful morning," Ige said. Sunlit turned to her free side to find that he *had* decided to walk up the beach with them. "Until Chip showed up, anyway."

"Actually, Chip was helpful," Sunlit said, biting her tongue before she added anything that might give away Chip's application plans.

"There's a first." Ige huffed.

Sunlit felt it was high time to change the subject, and since Fish and Chip were happily discussing lunch foods, she was on her own with Ige. "Speaking of helpful, how was Fish?"

"He was excellent." Ige softened, even smiled faintly. "He put the trainees through their paces."

"And there weren't any—um—incidents?" Sunlit wasn't sure what she was more worried about: Fish's unpredictable magic, or rude bystanders.

Ige met her gaze before he replied, and she knew he understood. "None. Everyone was too busy."

You kept them too busy, Sunlit concluded, reading between the lines. Her gratitude to Ige grew.

"About this lunch," he began—

"Don't worry about it," she interrupted. "I really did want to bring something to share. But I probably wouldn't have come up with anything as fancy as the deli. That was Chip's doing."

"I've seen what you think passes for a meal," Ige said, meditatively, as they climbed up on the boardwalk. "Maybe it *is* good that Chip went with you."

"Hey," Sunlit protested, taken by surprise.

"Hey," a new voice echoed—a stranger, standing just in front of the Sanctuary. "Hello? Are you Sunlit Haven? Oh, thank goodness. What good timing. We found these babies for you!"

17

An Official Check-in

> *The moon ray is very special. Its big, flat wings can glow!*
> *But it has to bask in the moon's light. Moon rays charge*
> *up their wings by swimming close to the surface. Then*
> *they dive deep under the waves to find their favorite*
> *foods!*
>   —*from* The Children's Encyclopedia of Deep Sea
> Creatures

They really were babies—of a marine variety, of course. Maternal instinct mingled with veterinary expertise, and Sunlit put her foot down, insisting that Fish remain with Chip and Ige to have lunch. As excited to care for their new charges as he was, he could easily hurt the little creatures. So, as soon as they made it inside the Sanctuary, she sent him out again.

"The sailor man was here earlier," said Joy to Sunlit, as the trio of Ige, Fish, and Chip departed to find a picnic spot on the boardwalk nearby. "Just come this way."

With agility that confounded Sunlit, the giant otter slipped over the sales counter and opened the back door. She was outside in a flash of brown fur. *I knew normal otters are acrobatic, but that is something else,* Sunlit thought. She decided not to wonder too much about how Joy could open doors or squeeze through tight spaces—particularly with a tail that still needed to be treated with care.

Besides, she had more pressing matters. The stranger outside the Sanctuary had been one of a local clamming operation, and they'd gifted Sunlit a new bucket. A new, extra-large bucket brimming with baby moon rays, each as flat and small and helpless as the palm of her hand.

Moving carefully with the heavy, rather unsteady burden, Sunlit followed Joy. She found that the otter had been absolutely right: while she was out, Pa had installed two new rope ladders down to the recovery pool, just as he'd promised. The one trailing down from the back door had wide plank steps and easily supported her and her precious cargo. Chip's father had even thought to install a bit of old pipe as a handrail.

The apple doesn't fall far from the tree, Sunlit thought, smiling to herself as she stepped down into the prow of the boat. *Or is there a more nautical version of the saying I should use?*

"Here," Joy called, from behind the boat's stern.

Sunlit made sure her hat was in place over her short hair, and then looked up. At the back of the boat, in the shallow water of the "shelf," the lion seal was sleeping peacefully. Over the rise and fall of his rounded side, Sunlit saw Joy, bobbing in the water with one paw on the boat and one paw around a large roll of gossamer netting, the kind a fishing boat might use to capture tiny krill.

"Joy!" Sunlit cried back, aghast. "Where did you get that?"

"Farther down the pier, stuck under the railing," Joy replied, hauling herself back onto the boat and scampering along its side like the feat meant nothing. Not so much as a drop of water disturbed the lion seal. Joy slunk down into the boat beside Sunlit, ripples in the shallow water the only evidence of her passing. She held out the netting for inspection proudly. "I could smell it the whole time I was out there waiting for you. Teeny little shrimps, or something like that—nothing I'd want to eat, myself, but good for someone, I suppose. It'd be sure to work for moon rays, don't you think?"

"They definitely couldn't get through the holes," Sunlit agreed. "But water still could. Which is a good thing, normally, but I'm still worried about the lion seal being contagious. Babies could be especially vulnerable to getting sick. I don't know for sure that they can catch what he has, but—"

"We certainly wouldn't take chances," Joy agreed, companionably. "That's why I thought you might want to use the barrel."

The—? Sunlit opened her mouth, but just as quickly shut it again. Somehow, the Sanctuary was turning out to be a force of nature—and so was Joy. She decided to give up on being incredulous for the moment. Instead, she smiled. "Lead on," she told Joy. "At this rate, I guess we really *had* better think about cleaning up the pier."

Sinuous and graceful, Joy glided to the back of the boat again, then up and over the side. Moving clunkily, making sure of each bootstep through the water, Sunlit followed. She edged carefully around the lion seal, which snorted in its sleep. Its mane, she was pleased to note, was looking much more full and majestic after a thorough wash yesterday.

Just as she peered over the back of the boat, Joy surfaced.

"Joy, isn't your tail hurting you?" Sunlit asked, unable to stop herself.

"Just a twinge now and then," the otter said. Her head and shoulders rose out of the water, and half of a humongous barrel floated in front of her. "See? Mister Daleson found this when he was putting in the second ladder for you."

"Mister—? Oh." Sunlit shook her head. *First 'the sailor man,' now 'mister.'* She wondered, vaguely, just how old Joy was. Could her habitual honorifics and descriptions be a sign of youth? It was hard to tell; Sunlit had no idea—in fact she was sure very few people did—how quickly a giant sea otter grew or how long one lived.

"It was bobbing in low tide," Joy was saying. "He told me to tell you we ought to fish it out, or it might harm the boat. But what if, instead, you tied it *to* the boat?"

Sunlit focused, thinking it over. It was a little alarming, how quickly the Sanctuary was growing. And yet, it really wasn't appropriate to keep the moon rays in one of the empty tanks inside the shop. They'd have to be split into groups in order to fit into the small fish tanks, first of all, and more importantly, moon rays thrived on the actual light of the moon, so they'd surely suffer inside a building.

The barrel, meanwhile, was easily big enough to hold all the baby rays. It could have held Sunlit twice over, as far as she could see. It had lost its iron rings and been split in two lengthwise, leaving a trough held together with interior wooden struts.

"I think the other half is wedged at the bottom," Joy added, her nose pointing over her shoulder at the sea along the breakwater.

"Are there any holes in this half?" Sunlit asked. It didn't matter too much—she could line it with the netting if she needed to. Still, it was good to know how much work they were in for.

"I don't feel any," said Joy. "Want to see the other half too?"

"Please," Sunlit decided.

In no time at all, Joy fished up the rest of the barrel. Together, end to end, the barrels were nearly as long as the back of the boat. Seeing this clenched the deal for Sunlit. She set about lashing the barrel halves together, with Joy's help for the underwater parts. There was just enough rope leftover to secure the barrels to the boat, if loosely.

"Mister Daleson could use his tools on it if you asked him," Joy suggested, blowing bubbles in the waves.

"I might," Sunlit admitted. "But it's good for the moment. Let's get these little critters out of this bucket."

They filled one barrel half with the moon rays, which quickly settled along the wood at the bottom. This was normal behavior for a moon ray during the day, and it gratified Sunlit greatly. Apparently, the clammers had found the babies inside one of their less-used skiffs, perhaps driven there by the storm days ago. Sunlit was glad that their strange circumstances hadn't hindered the babies' instincts.

To make sure they were safe from predators—and from too much sun—Sunlit stretched the netting atop the barrel. Joy gladly sliced what they needed with her teeth. Pieces of oyster shells helped wedge the corners of the netting in place against the rough wood along the upper edge of the barrels. The two had just finished and Sunlit was about to congratulate her furry assistant when she heard a voice from above.

"Hard at work, then? Good, good! I'll tell the council all

about it."

Sunlit squinted up to see Taiwo grinning widely down at them. "Are you here on official business? Sorry we weren't at the shop to meet you."

"Don't you worry. Chip and Fish are up there. I take it my brother stormed off, as he is wont to do," Taiwo said lightly. "But I *am* here on business, as a matter of fact. I don't want to take you away from whatever important thing you're doing, but if you're done, could you spare a moment?"

Sunlit glanced at Joy, and nodded. Whatever Taiwo and the town council wanted, she wasn't going to turn them down.

* * *

"Have you thought about cleaning up the pier?" was Taiwo's first question as they took seats along the side of the Sanctuary. Chip played pickup-sticks with Fish nearby.

Sunlit, momentarily distracted by the fact that the Sanctuary now had a bench next to the side door, stuttered. "I, um, I was just thinking about that."

Joy slid past them, intensely interested in the game of sticks. Sunlit thought about asking the three of them to move into the shade, but Fish looked perfectly cool and happy, and Taiwo was still talking.

"It's your property so you can do what you like, of course," they were saying, "but it would definitely curry favor with the rest of the council."

"Do I need to do that?" Sunlit refocused on Taiwo's deep purple eyes. "Curry favor, I mean?"

Taiwo shrugged, a fluid and expressive movement. "The conversation about Fish is settled as far as we're concerned, for the moment at least. But Clementina is by no means done with her complaints—if she *ever* is—that's just between you and me. Fish seems to have made a bad impression on her, but trust me, everything makes a bad impression on her."

Despite this assurance, Sunlit winced, thinking of the lady they'd soaked on the boardwalk.

"It may be a different matter once we start looking at applications," Taiwo went on. "But in terms of currying favor, I was thinking more about the future of your little marine center here. What are you going to call it?"

"Oh, we've been calling it the Sanctuary," Sunlit said. She couldn't recall when exactly that had started. "Marine Sanctuary."

"I love it," Taiwo declared. "Have you thought about getting a sign? How are the protection spells holding up?"

"Oh, um." Sunlit looked over her shoulder at the building behind them, as though it might know the answer better than she did. "I really hadn't thought about a sign. Or, um, any more documents that need to be done?"

"You leave the boring stuff to me," Taiwo said, with confidence. "I can't tell you how long I've been waiting for something *amazing* like this to take over this old eyesore. But it won't do much good if it all gets swept away in the next storm, right?"

"Right, the protection spells." Sunlit tried to think. "I haven't really noticed. I'm not too good with that kind of thing. We haven't had any problems, but we do have more animals now, and I really wouldn't want them in danger."

"I can get the town Witch to come over," Taiwo offered.

Sunlit replied without filtering herself. "No, that's okay."

"No?" Taiwo followed Sunlit's gaze to where Fish was

arguing with Chip about a messy pile of sticks. "I see. You know . . ."

Taiwo reached out their hand, placing it delicately on Sunlit's sleeve. In a voice much gentler than their usual up-beat, let's-get-things-done tones, they said, "Seaside can be reactionary at times, but I've seen that things do work out. We went through it when we established the merfolk camp offshore, and when I married Rei. On top of that, I have to say, I've never seen Ige this involved with someone who wasn't either directly working for him or running around with a fishing boat and a tail. And I know he has great judgment these days, even if he is still *too* judgy at times."

"Ige?" In looking down at the iridescent mer-scales on Taiwo's dark hand, Sunlit noticed the faded paint on the bench they were using. It was the same red and white as the lifeguard station. "He's been great," she said thickly. "A lot of people have. It's just . . ."

"Never mind the 'just,'" said Taiwo, smiling with more of their usual energy. "The people who matter want the Sanctuary, and Fish, to stay for a good long time. And in the meantime, I bet more people than you'd suspect would be willing to help you clean up the pier."

"It would be good to get it done," Sunlit said absently.

"How about tomorrow? I can help spread the word," Taiwo said briskly, standing. "I'm just off to a meeting with Rei and the boardwalk shop owners now. They'd probably be more than glad to lend a hand."

"I don't know about that," said Sunlit, thinking of Coral. "But . . . sure. The sooner the better. Thank you."

Then she'd have some more good news to write back to Professor McAlpin about. Surely she was done with her conference now, and would be happy to read about the pier and respond?

"No need," Taiwo assured her, their white teeth flashing in a broad grin. "Like I said, I've been hoping for an opportunity like this for a long time. Plus, anything that gets Ige off that dratted lifeguard stand is a good idea, in my book!"

18

A Tactless Spill

While notable for its ring of sand and bright coloring, the saturn snail is also interesting for its mating habits. Unlike other snails, the saturn snail selects its mate very carefully. Two snails' rings must align perfectly before they commence the mating dance . . .

—*from* Traverse's Guide to Marine Vertebrates, Invertebrates, and Magical Outliers

Around tea time, Sunlit finally managed to have lunch. Joy, who despite her protestations had worked a little too hard that morning, slept curled up in the Sanctuary. Fish was asleep too, holding on to his life jacket, leaning against Joy's furry side. His snores were a small, faint echo of Joy's.

"Thank you for looking after him while Taiwo was here," Sunlit said quietly to Chip. She'd elected to stay outside on the bench, which was shaded by the shop.

Chip stretched his legs out across the boardwalk from where he sat against the door frame beside her. "You act like it's some kind of trouble. What better thing could I do with my day off?"

"You're either endlessly nice, or you really do like Fish a lot," Sunlit said, popping bread and cheese in her mouth. It took her several seconds to realize she'd said it aloud.

Her cheeks burned with embarrassment, but Chip, after one shocked moment, laughed. "Maybe both? I won't turn down a compliment. But the little kid really does grow on you."

"He does," Sunlit said, swallowing her shame. "Have you always liked children?"

"I guess I never really noticed before," said Chip, thoughtfully. He reached up for another bottle of lemonade from the basket beside Sunlit and went on, "There's not a lot of kids out on the fishing boats. And I knew from a young age I wouldn't be making kids the usual way, if you catch my drift."

Sunlit had not, as of yet, given any thought to Chip's sexuality. After years working with undergraduate students—and their particular penchant for drama—she'd essentially trained herself not to wonder about such things. But she took this in stride, nodding. It certainly wasn't unusual.

"Pa said last night that sometimes, you don't realize you might be ready until you *are*," Chip added. At this, he paused, taking a sip of his lemonade.

To Sunlit, this silence seemed out of character. And compared with the yelling families on the beach and the snores from inside the Sanctuary, it was loud. After a moment, she decided to say something. "But you still seem a little worried?"

"Not about Fish," Chip said. "But yeah, you could say so. It's just the whole application thing."

"What about it?" Sunlit smeared jam on another piece of

bread. Now that she'd started eating, it was hard to stop. "Did you talk to Taiwo just now?"

"I did, before they went and found you on the pier," Chip admitted. "That's kind of what worries me. I could have sworn that when I said Pa and I would apply, they got a strange glint in their eye."

"Are you sure Taiwo doesn't just *always* have a glint?" Sunlit asked, speculating on her own experiences with the council representative so far. Taiwo definitely seemed the type who had their own agenda at all times . . . But it seemed like their agenda was a good one. Mostly. Probably.

"You're not wrong." Chip chuckled despite himself. "But, I don't know, this one seemed different. Maybe I'm just sensitive. But basically the very next thing they said had to do with Ige and asking if he'd been by."

Sunlit considered digging into some carrots and hummus. "You think Taiwo's going to tell Ige? That *was* what you were worried about earlier, right?"

"I figured there was no stopping it getting back to him eventually." Chip sighed, looking out toward the beach without truly focusing on anything. "But now that he probably *does* know, I feel like I'm waiting for the other shoe to drop. I swear he hates me, Sunlit. He'll sabotage it somehow."

Sunlit spent one moment munching on a carrot straw, contemplating being her usual, close-mouthed self. But from start to finish, everything about what Chip had said was pulling her to speak.

"I'm sorry, Chip," she said at last. "But that's absolutely ridiculous."

Chip spat out lemonade. "Wow, tell me how you *really* feel, Professor."

"It is, though," said Sunlit. She was gaining steam now, sitting up, carrot forgotten. "It's absolute nonsense. Rubbish. I can't believe I'm talking to the same person who recognized the immediate need for outside help for a giant otter and took sensible action to save its life."

"Ouch! You're making me regret that a little bit now," Chip said, shifting to look up at her squarely.

"Well, you deserve it." Sunlit remained firm, looking back down as though he was one of her students. "What basis do you have to say Ige hates you?"

"You've seen him," Chip protested. "He's always yelling at me. All I have to do is walk by, and somehow suddenly I'm walking wrong."

"And does he yell like that at anyone else?" Sunlit asked.

"No," Chip said, sulkily. "It's the worst. I don't even know what I did."

Sunlit could see that her pupil was not going to arrive at a new conclusion on his own. She was going to have to come right out and say it. "Has it occurred to you that he treats you differently because he *loves* you?"

For a whole minute, Chip was silent.

Then he blinked. "You should stick to animals, Professor."

"I'm serious," Sunlit protested, leaning in. "Just think about it. Maybe he's really *worried* about you. I mean, boating next to the pier, carrying huge carpets around, holding your breath for too long—you can kind of see *why* he might worry, can't you?"

"I've kept myself alive just fine for this long," Chip retorted. "And anyway, that's a terrible way of telling someone you love them. I'm half convinced he *can't* love people, based on the way he acts!"

"I'm not saying it's all that clever or romantic," Sunlit conceded. "But we are talking about Ige, here."

Chip hesitated, his head at an angle, ears cocked. "Well—you do have a point there."

"The only thing either of you can talk about for more than two minutes is each other," Sunlit added. She dug through the basket and found a few stalks of celery, which she promptly dipped into the hummus, too. "Until Fish came along, at least."

"Hey, that's not fair. We talked about your troubles this morning," Chip reminded her.

"So now it's your turn," Sunlit replied matter-of-factly. "Why don't you just tell him how you feel?"

"Because it's Ige," Chip complained. "Also, I haven't admitted to feeling anything. Except annoyed."

"Have it your own way, then." Sunlit settled back down, her carrots and celery gone. She took another look at the picnic basket. She felt strangely exhilarated, having spoken her mind.

Chip nursed the rest of his lemonade, looking out over the beach. In the shop behind them, Fish stirred and mumbled in his sleep. Joy continued to snore.

"Where's your bird?" Chip asked suddenly.

"I don't know," Sunlit admitted, through a mouthful of bread and honey. "He's never far away from food, though. He's probably on the roof, or . . ."

She looked back into the shop, and Chip followed her gaze. As one, they noticed the blue parrot balanced on the register at the far end.

Biscuit noticed them looking at him and flapped his wings. *"I'm applying! Ige hates me!"*

"So much for him not overhearing your secrets," Sunlit told Chip, grinning despite herself.

"Maybe it's Biscuit who hates me," Chip agreed, though he was grinning too. "Oh well. It's too late now! Hear that, bird?"

Joy startled and woke up, blinking heavily. "What'd I miss?"

"Just a misguided romance," Sunlit said, chuckling.

Joy flopped her head back onto the floor and fell asleep once more.

* * *

The next morning, Sunlit nearly overslept.

At first, she didn't even mind. She stretched in her cot and admired the early glow cast from the windows. But then she remembered that she had a barrel full of baby moon rays to look after, on top of her other creatures. They needed special food; unlike most other kinds of ray, moon rays ate a strictly vegetarian diet. That meant extra time for food preparation had to be built into her morning schedule.

And she'd promised Taiwo to clean up the pier.

She sat bolt upright, thinking. Surely no one would come? Everyone had better things to do. But if no one came, how could she hope to get the job done? She had Fish to look after, and she did not want Joy to overdo it again today.

And if they *did* come, what then? She had no work gloves or safety gear to provide them.

There was the extra sunscreen and water pouches from the lifeguards, of course . . .

But who was she kidding? No one would come. Most of them were probably terrified of Fish, like the tourists at Coral's Consignment. They hadn't even seen him and they were still scared. Surely people wouldn't come to where he was known to be staying.

Of course, Arietta and Chip and Ige and Pa didn't mind . . . but she couldn't let them clean up an entire pier for her sake. Especially since they all had their own work to do.

Maybe if she worked *really* fast, she could get most of it done before anyone else woke up?

Sunlit washed and dressed in record time, with record levels of quietness. Fish was sleeping heavily in his cot by the ocean rug, and she wanted him to stay that way for as long as possible. He'd had a big day yesterday, after all, with lots of time in the sun.

The sun—Sunlit grabbed her heaviest shirt and overalls. If she did everything this morning, the heat wouldn't be so bad . .
.

But should she feed the animals first? The salamander tended to get grumpy if breakfast was late. But the crab would probably be okay with waiting. And the lion seal had yet to eat very much at all. Still, he would need another dose of medicine, and she wanted to be sure a meal was waiting for him once he was ready
. . .

Was there time?

What if Biscuit squawked and gave her away?

Sunlit hopped down to the first floor, having barely touched the ladder. She landed as softly as possible in her boots, her heart beating loud in the darkness.

But should she go out the back door, to the boat?

Or make the animals' food?

Or go around the side, to the pier, and get right to work?

She stood, paralyzed by indecision and worry . . .

Until someone gave a polite, whiskered cough behind her. "Oh, Sunlit, you're up—wonderful," said Joy. "They'll want to talk to you, I'm sure."

"They? Who's they?" Sunlit asked, turning as slowly and creakily as if she was a character in a campfire ghost story.

"*Cleanup the pier!*" squawked Biscuit, from atop the fish tanks. "*Tell the town!*"

"Everybody," said Joy, with great satisfaction. "I told them to set up breakfast right outside. Can you believe no one thought to bring fish? But it's alright. I caught some of my own this morning. Nothing tastes quite as good as food you caught yourself . . ."

Joy kept talking, but Sunlit heard very little. She moved toward the side door as though swimming through a dream.

And at the door itself, she hesitated.

Joy, twisty and curly as an eel, curved around her and put her head over Sunlit's shoulder. "What's the matter? Aren't you happy to see your friends?"

"Joy," said Sunlit, very low and hoarse, "I'm worried."

"Yes, you do that a lot," Joy agreed. "And you never ask directly for help. Did you know that?"

"I don't know," said Sunlit.

"But even so, your friends want to help you," Joy added, not cruelly or judgmentally, but in a light and interested tone. "It's really a very nice thing. Don't you think?"

Sunlit licked her lips. "I'm not sure."

"I am," Joy said, firmly. "Time to get out in the water, kit."

And with a giant otter pressing its nose into the small of her back, Sunlit had very little option but to open the door.

19

A Further Step

Merfolk aren't creatures, they're people like you and me. But they like to live in the sea. Some live in very deep water. Some travel across whole oceans. Each clan of merfolk is different. If you ever get invited to a merfolk camp or city, make sure you go!
—from The Children's Encyclopedia of Deep Sea Creatures

"Why didn't you tell me about the cleanup?" Chip was the first person Sunlit saw, and he immediately had a friendly arm around her shoulders. "I nearly went out on the boat and missed it!"

"Didn't I tell you?" Sunlit mumbled, as she took a good look around.

The boardwalk next to Marine Sanctuary was entirely taken over. Taiwo was on hand, overseeing the erection of a large canvas tent. In its shadow, several picnic tables had been set up, and Arietta was shaking tablecloths over them with practiced ease. A group of strangers, most likely sailors, loitered nearby, waiting for a cart full of pastries to be opened up and distributed.

"I brought the crew along," Chip said cheerfully. "The more the merrier, right?"

Sunlit had never fully understood this phrase.

Further along, where the boardwalk met the old pier, a group of merfolk lingered. There were perhaps half a dozen, most with the same dark skin and blue or purple scales as Taiwo and Ige. Seeing Sunlit's glance, one of them separated from the group and came over.

"I'm Jeannie," she said, extending one graceful hand. "Taiwo and Ige have told me so much about you, Sunlit Haven. And you, Joy. I'm glad to meet you both. It's good to see you so well, also, Chip."

"Hey, Jeannie," Chip said pleasantly. To Sunlit, he added, "Jeannie is Taiwo and Ige's mom, and basically runs the Afolayan merfolk camp out from shore. She got all the charm and beauty in the family and she kept it to herself."

"Stop that, young man." Jeannie laughed, her air friendly and relaxed. Her flowing, fashionable tunic and tightly braided hair echoed Taiwo's style, while her eyes were deep blue like Ige's—without the hint of derision his often had. It made Sunlit untense just to be around her. Indeed, Jeannie's smile was more effective than any anti-anxiety medicine Sunlit could think of, as she turned and continued, "We've been admiring your creative annex, dear. Such a clever use of old debris."

Annex—the perfect name for the wrecked boat-turned-recovery pool! Sunlit perked up further. "Thank you so much!

It wasn't just my idea. We've all been working on it."

"It was my idea to add the barrels," Joy said, over Sunlit's shoulder.

"I can't wait to see what you do with the rest of the pier and its contents," Jeannie told them. "When Taiwo recruited us to your cause, it came at the perfect time. We've been wondering how we could help our landfolk neighbors after the storm."

"Helping the Sanctuary helps everyone on the beach, especially the critters. Isn't that right, Sunlit?" Chip nudged her.

"I—I guess that is the idea," she admitted, somewhat surprised. "I wasn't sure what to expect, in terms of help. I hope you aren't disappointed."

Jeannie exchanged a knowing glance with Chip before smiling at Sunlit again. "I'd advise you to put thoughts of disappointment from your head, dear. The important thing is that we've come together to make a little change."

There was that word again, *together.* It seemed strange to Sunlit that everyone in Seaside would leap to use it, when the truth was that she was probably going to leave soon.

But if they're invested in the Sanctuary, then they can help keep it going while the University decides what to do, she told herself. This made her feel a little more confident.

"So this is the new Marine Sanctuary, hm?" a new voice said.

Sunlit spun, leaving Chip and Joy to continue talking to Jeannie. From the boardwalk, Rachel was approaching her and her shop. Her scholar's robe brushed the tops of her bright pink strappy sandals, which matched her pink glasses. She put her hands on her hips and singled out Sunlit amid the bustle. "Looks pretty good for someone who just got here."

"I—I can't take all the credit," Sunlit stammered. She could hardly believe her eyes. *Rachel* had come to help with the work day?

Rachel smiled. "People like to help when something new and different comes along. I'm no exception. Here, I brought you some pamphlets on animal care that I found lying around the bookstore. They're probably ancient and out of date, but I thought you might be able to hand them out to tourists. Or sell them, even, and make some extra money."

"Thank you," said Sunlit reverently. As she accepted the bundle of folded parchment, another thought came to her. "We should probably have standard intake forms and things, for the Sanctuary. I don't know if you do things like that . . ."

"I can help you set up a template, for sure." Rachel's smile deepened. "It'd be the least I can do, especially since I can't stay to help today."

"Oh—you aren't staying?" Sunlit tried not to sound too disappointed.

"I have to open my shop," Rachel explained. "I don't have any help at the moment. But I wanted to come by first and give you those pamphlets—and say good luck. It's really about time something like this came to Seaside, you know?"

Sunlit beamed as Rachel took her leave. Suddenly, the crowd around the Sanctuary was much less daunting. The pier itself was much less daunting. In fact, nothing at all seemed very daunting in that moment.

And just like that, barely seven days after she'd first arrived, Sunlit Haven was leading an official clean up effort on the pier.

It started with more good humor, jocular introductions, and Arietta's lovely baking. When Fish and Biscuit tumbled out of the shop to find them, there was a moment of silence—and then everyone continued on as usual.

"Come on, kiddo, did you eat yet?" Chip said, immediately

taking Fish under his wing.

"I'm a wild kelpie from a big herd of kelpies!" Fish told him excitedly as they moved through the crowd. Fish, unbeknownst to Sunlit, had spent a good portion of last evening poring over the pictures in his new book.

Sunlit watched the two head for a table, willing her butterflies to calm down. Taiwo showed up at her side and leaned in.

"If anyone was worried about curses, I told them not to come," they said quietly.

"Thank you," Sunlit said, surprised once more.

"And look how many *did* come," Taiwo added meaningfully, before being pulled into yet another conversation.

There were, in fact, enough people to have several work crews. Several of the merfolk volunteered for sea duty, swimming along underneath the pier to catch debris or help dislodge stubborn planks from below. Jeannie and a few others opted to dive deeper, investigating the columns the pier rested on for evidence of damage. This particular task made Sunlit more nervous than she'd expected—if any of the supports were damaged beyond repair, that would mean serious rebuilding was needed to maintain the pier, and she wasn't sure how she could handle that. So she was secretly relieved Jeannie was leading that team. Something about Jeannie and her judgment seemed implicitly trustworthy and fair.

Meanwhile, above the waves, no one was slouching either. Taiwo took over the duty of watching over the annex, with its lion seal and baby rays, to make sure no one was disturbed. Sunlit suspected this was mostly so that Taiwo could remain in the thick of the action and ready to talk to anyone who came by, but she was appreciative, nonetheless. Chip led the sailors and other "landfolk" helpers, who grabbed burlap sacks and began moving down the pier, cleaning or removing obstacles as they went. Arietta said she had enough pastries left under the tent that she intended to run her bakery from there, with Fish's help.

All of which left Sunlit and Joy staring at one another.

"Actually, there is one other thing I think we should do," said Sunlit, slowly.

"There's a good kit. Lead me to it," said Joy, affably. "With me helping, you'll be able to get it done in the flick of a tail."

* * *

Progress wasn't *quite* as quick as an otter's tail might be, but to Sunlit, it was downright magical.

She and Joy returned to the bakery tent at lunch time, to find the place bustling. Between Arietta's temporary "pop up" bakery stand and Taiwo's willingness to engage every passing tourist in conversation, many newcomers had been recruited to the cause. Some merely helped move a beam or sweep up a corner, but others joined the fray and stayed.

One such constant was Chip's father, Pa. He'd apparently taken up residence on a stool under the tent across from Arietta, and there he was directing volunteers who came off the pier carrying debris. He was sorting it all into piles: burlap sacks of "junk," a barrel full of scrap iron, hooks, and nails, another barrel of pieces of rope, an uncertain heap of "possibly useful" items, and a neat stack of lumber that could be reused.

"This is incredible," Sunlit said, looking at the organized piles all lined up along the side of the Sanctuary. They'd entirely covered up her new bench, but that was perfectly fine: she hadn't even realized how many useful things were still out on the wrecked pier. The scrap iron in particular might as well have been a heap of gold, as far as she was concerned. She knew she could get good money for it at the market.

When she mentioned this aloud to Pa, he chuckled. "Aye, most never know what they have under the mess. Not so worried about your purchase now, I hope?"

"Worried!" Sunlit glanced around and, seeing that Joy and Fish were occupied and no one nearby was eyeing Pa's extra stool, she claimed it. Lifting her hat to wipe her brow, she confided in Pa, "When you think about it, this really is an ideal setup for a Marine Center. It just needs a *lot* of work."

"You got a lot of helpers," Pa observed, waving another sailor with an armful of chain links toward the iron barrel. "Need some more skill soon, though. That railing, for instance."

Sunlit followed his glance out at the pier. While the others cleared and cleaned, she and Joy had been working along the rail, righting the beams and fixing what they could. It now looked much more respectable, but there were still gaps where the railing had been crushed, and Sunlit knew firsthand that some of the upright beams were still wobbly.

"The barrels on the annex, too," Sunlit admitted. "We do need someone good with a hammer and nails, at least. I've never really done that myself. Joy seemed to think . . ."

"Aye," said Pa, contentedly. "I'll come by tomorrow. Just be in the way, today."

"We'd really appreciate it," Sunlit said, touched.

"Appreciate this tent." With practiced ease, Pa deflected the gratitude. To Sunlit, it was a familiar move. When he did it, it made her grin.

"Taiwo's idea, I think, but a very good one," she admitted.

"You got sense, keeping the sun off you," Pa added, nodding

at her hat and sleeves.

Sunlit looked down at them too. She rarely heard people *compliment* her fashion choices.

"Yeah, well," she said, deciding not to get into the whole burning thing. For something that had often felt like her own kind of curse, it seemed rather small at the moment. "Turns out it's nice to have protection when we're dealing with splintered wood, too."

"Sunlit, did you see this?" Joy had slipped over to the "possibly useful" junk pile, her whiskers twitching. With deft paws, she unearthed part of a string of magical fairy lanterns. "We could put this along the railings and brighten things up!"

"Literally," Sunlit agreed, smiling. "That's not a bad idea. I wonder where they came from?"

"Strange things come from the sea," Pa said knowingly. He glanced at Sunlit. "Jeannie say anything about the boy?"

"Fish? Not to me," Sunlit said. She glanced over her shoulder. Fish was still helping Arietta sell things, but now, they weren't just selling baked goods—they were selling the sunscreen potion and water pouches from the lifeguards, too. They were drawing steady business from boardwalk visitors and volunteers alike. "If she knew anything, though, she would have told Taiwo, right?"

"Like as not," Pa agreed. "Just wondered."

"Have lunch, so that we can get back to work," Joy urged.

Sunlit chuckled. "I will, but you really should rest, Joy."

"I've had enough rest to last me a lifetime," Joy declared.

Pa squinted at her. "Wait til you're old. See what you think."

"Age is just a number," Joy retorted, "and unless we're counting up fish, I don't have much use for those."

At this, Sunlit laughed—earnestly.

20

A Completed Task

> *There's nothing that can't be fixed up with a little string and tape, that's what I always say. And if you've got some magical glue and an extra pair of hands, even better. The only time this doesn't hold true is with matters of the heart . . . I'm still waiting on the day when they figure out how to patch those up in reasonable time.*
> —*from* I'm An Adventurer Here Myself

Work slowed as the afternoon reached its hottest point. The pier was clean enough then that many volunteers chose to run and leap from its end, cooling off with a swim. Now that the largest debris was out of the way, the verdict seemed clear: the pier was safe to use, but considerably shorter than it once had been, stretching out only halfway along the breakwater. It was plenty big enough to shield the annex and perhaps a few more annexes—room for many patients in the future . . .

Not, of course, Sunlit reminded herself, that *she* would be the one to look after them all. She was hardly qualified, was she?

As she and Fish tidied up the leftover pastries, a familiar face came walking up.

"Kelpies love donuts," Fish was telling Sunlit.

"Everybody loves donuts, don't they?" The vaguely familiar speaker wasn't one of the volunteers, and it took Sunlit a moment to place her. Frizzy red hair, bright green eyes, a floral sundress, wrinkles from laughter and smiles, a slightly stooping posture. The woman chuckled at Sunlit's obvious confusion—in friendly, forgiving manner. "Hard to recognize me without a kid in tow, isn't it? I feel like I'm never without them these days. But they're all at a summer play rehearsal, bless them—every single one. Their grandparents took them and I have a night to myself. And what could I think of to do, except to check on my eldest's fish?"

"Fish!" Sunlit said, putting the pieces together.

"What?" Fish asked, curious.

"No, Spick and Spann, the alpha fish," Sunlit explained. She returned the weary mother's smile. "It was just a case of stress and exhaustion. They've recovered very nicely with a few days of quiet. We've liked looking after them, haven't we?"

"They're very pretty," Fish told the woman seriously.

"And of course, I told you their names but I didn't leave mine, did I?" The woman shook her head with a rueful shrug. "I'm Leila."

"Sunlit," said Sunlit, but then she blushed. "I guess you already knew that. We have your bowl, too."

"You're a wonder," said Leila, smiling. "Do you trust me to take the critters home, then? The kids've been asking for them. They've been missed, let me tell you!"

"I'm sure they'd love to go home," Sunlit assured her. "Just let me ask, what do you have them in now?"

"An old glass cauldron," Leila answered, leaning against the table for a comfortable chat. "Used to be iron, of course, but one of the kids was working on transformation skills at school and had a bit of a mishap. The teacher sent the cauldron home, since they could hardly use it for potions any more. At first I thought, where in Beyond am I going to keep this? But then my eldest won the fish at a fair—and then it came in handy!"

"That's kind of what I thought." Sunlit smiled, happy to have been right and to have a solution to offer. "If you could just give them a bit of a lid, something that still lets air in but gives them some insulation—even a bit of canvas, or wood—that should keep them more comfortable. It's just the noise, I think, that was getting to them."

"The noise! It gets to me too," Leila confessed, grinning. "That makes perfect sense, doctor. I promise you it'll be done. With luck, you won't see Spick and Spann again!"

"We'd be happy to see them if they do need something, though," Sunlit said automatically. Just as she was regretting it, feeling she'd spoken awkwardly, Leila leaned closer.

"You should come over some time," she said to Sunlit. Her eyes were very kind. "We can compare notes."

She dipped her shoulder at Fish, and before Sunlit could protest, Fish himself piped up.

"What's notes?"

Leila laughed. "You'll find out soon enough, child. How old are you?"

"I'm a kelpie," Fish informed her. "They live forever."

"That's as may be, but even kelpies have to go to school," Leila told him. To Sunlit, she added, "I have one starting school this fall, too. I'm sure they'll be the best of friends. She just *loves* horses. Even a magical half-horse kelpie will do, I expect."

"We'll see what stays the same between now and then," Sunlit said, reluctantly—a little fearfully.

"I hear you." Leila's gaze was understanding and sweet. "Sometimes it seems like nothing can keep still for even a minute. That's why we have to take some time for ourselves, right? Maybe look after each other a bit."

"I . . . I suppose . . ."

"And speaking of, I owe you for Spick and Spann," Leila said, drawing a coin purse out of a deep pocket. "What are your rates?"

"I hadn't even thought about it," Sunlit admitted honestly. *That could be another thing to get Rachel's help with,* she thought. *We could make a reference sheet, or a board to hang by the register . . .*

"Let's call it a consultation fee, plus several nights' room and board," Leila suggested, setting coins down one by one as she spoke. When Fish stirred, interested, she gave the final two to him. "And if you need more, you can find me on Seagull Lane. Third house on the right, purple door, kids' bikes on the lawn. You can't miss it."

"Thank you," Sunlit stammered. "I'm sure this is fine. It's great. Thank you."

"But now we have to give her fish back?" Fish asked, looking up from his coins.

"Oh, right." Sunlit smiled apologetically at Leila as she rose. "I can bring them right out."

"Take your time," Leila told her. And as Sunlit turned away, Leila squatted down beside Fish, and she heard her say, "So tell me more about kelpies. Do they really lure people into the water like everyone says?"

"*I* wouldn't. Sunlit said not everyone likes water, so you have to ask first," Fish said.

Sunlit smiled to herself, her shoulders untensing just a little more.

* * *

Sunlit sent Spick and Spann home gladly, though she felt a little bereft doing so. She knew, from her practical experience, that the fish were recovered and would be fine; but she still had never gotten that 'feeling' from them. Somehow, in her work at the Marine Center, she had relied on it more than she'd realized. She missed the confidence it gave her.

She also felt a twinge about the invitation Leila had extended. Sunlit got the feeling—a decidedly unmagical feeling, but a persistent feeling nonetheless—that Leila had meant it. And she felt very bad, indeed a bit regretful too, that she wouldn't be taking her up on the offer.

The solution, Sunlit decided, was to throw herself into her work. The sun was slowly beginning to set, and the breeze from the ocean was cooling; the volunteers that remained had resumed their cleanup efforts. They swept and tidied the pier, and some of the sailors had rustled up a hammer and nails, with which they were reinforcing the railing under Pa's watchful eye. Jeannie was holding council with the other merfolk, their heads just visible over the waves as they treaded water, chatting in an easy circle. When she saw Sunlit walking nearby, Jeannie waved.

"Sunlit, dear," she called. "We just finished fixing up your pier."

"You—you did?" Sunlit walked over to the nearest section of finished railing and leaned on it. She'd expected them to inspect the pier from underwater, but not to get the work done already, too.

Jeannie's smile was visible even at a distance. "Have you ever seen merfolk at work?"

"I . . . No, I haven't," Sunlit admitted.

"I don't know much about how the other clans do it, of course," Jeannie said. "It may be different over in New West Key. But here, we make use of the sand around us. We use the magic of the ocean itself to form new structures."

"Or reinforce old ones," a nearby merperson added, grinning.

Like the saturn snail, Sunlit thought. She'd never known that merfolk could do such a thing. For a moment, she wondered if the University had employed any merfolk when they'd built the Marine Center. It was an impressive building, state of the art, and yet . . .

And yet, it doesn't have as many different people behind it as the Sanctuary does, Sunlit couldn't help but think.

She set aside the little bit of pride and focused on gratitude. "Jeannie, all of you, thank you so much. I can't believe you did so much. I wish I had something to offer you."

"Looking after the animals is enough," one of the merfolk said.

Jeannie nodded. "We wanted to help the town recover, and now we have. We are satisfied, Sunlit. And now, your pier will stand for many more years to come."

"Thank you," was all Sunlit could say.

Jeannie smiled one more time as, around her, heads began to disappear under the waves. "We're returning to our camp now, dear, but please, don't hesitate to send word if you need our help again. In fact, you can come and see the camp for yourself—there's a ferry that leaves from the marina. Come any time you like. And tell Taiwo I said to come visit too, won't you?"

Sunlit nodded and waved, still half dazzled. Then she turned and joined the fray on the pier just in time to assist Joy in stringing up her fairy lights. At the end of the pier the railing crew had left a purposeful gap for people going down to—or coming up from—the water. It was a perfect spot for another of Pa's ladders. To one side of the gap, Sunlit helped Joy tie her first string of lights, which stretched down the end of the pier and turned along the side. While Joy carefully looped the strand over the railing, Sunlit followed along, twisting the lights so they fell into place in an orderly fashion.

And as evening took hold, the lights began to glow.

"This looks perfect," Taiwo declared.

Sunlit straightened up from the railing, where she'd affixed tied the free end of their last light strand. Where the pier met the boardwalk there was now a rough gate—some of the leftover wood and two old oars, which swung to meet each other in the middle of the pier. At either end, they were held in place by hinges from the barrel of iron scraps. An old bit of chain dangled from one side so that the two halves of the gate could be secured closed. It was, indeed, perfect.

But now, the pier and nearby boardwalk were quiet—save for Taiwo, who had snuck up on Sunlit and Joy with uncharacteristic stealth.

"It really did clean up well," Joy declared. "Did you see they even patched the hole near where my boat was?"

"I did, and I approve wholeheartedly," said Taiwo, grinning. "So does the council. I was just off to report to them, and to catch up on town business."

"Really? You left and came back?" Sunlit felt somewhat chagrined for not noticing.

"And brought back dinner," Taiwo informed her, totally unperturbed. "It's under the tent. You'd better go and get some quick before everyone eats it all—it's from the taco place; Rei knows the guy who owns it, and he owed us a favor."

"Oh, okay," Sunlit said, looking over at Joy. *More favors, hmm?* "I guess it *is* dinner time—"

"But first," said Taiwo, interrupting them before they could head for the food, "maybe we should talk about something."

"Something? From the council?" Sunlit froze. "Is it—do they need to inspect the pier? Is it Clementina?"

"Officer Ebb'll be by tomorrow to give it an official look, but I'm sure it's fine. Especially since it's actually your property," Taiwo reminded her.

"Right," said Sunlit, uncertainly. Joy nudged her.

"We've done marvelous work, kit," the otter said.

Sunlit was reminded that *kit* was the word for otter babies. *Perhaps Joy really is older than she seems . . .*

. . . And she thinks I am being childish. Sunlit sighed and refocused. "Was there something else, then, Taiwo?"

"There was." The councilperson hesitated, for perhaps the first time ever. "Sunlit, ah, I just wanted to be the one to tell you. Quietly, at first."

What is it? Sunlit's anxiety kicked into gear once more. *Is the university not actually allowed out here? Did they contact the town without letting me know and turn the place down? Is that why Professor McAlpin hasn't been returning my letters? Does she know something she just doesn't want to say?*

"It's about Fish," said Taiwo, slowly. "While I was in session with the council earlier, we looked over the applications and took a vote."

"The—applications?" Sunlit was caught off guard. Hers was still rolled up under the sales counter. Had she missed her chance? Had she wanted that chance? "I didn't realize they were due so soon."

"We left them open on a rolling basis, but we kind of figured, the right fit would turn up sooner rather than later," Taiwo said. "That's usually how it seems to go. We wanted someone who was certain, you know, not someone who delayed too long about deciding."

"But they might need time to prepare," Sunlit blurted out. "Maybe they had to check a few things, or get approval from someone else in their family, or—or—"

Taiwo was looking at her a little strangely. "If that was the case, of course, someone could bring it up with the council when the decision is posted publicly tomorrow."

"You decided?" Sunlit felt faint. "Did you have many applications?"

"We had the one that mattered." Taiwo sounded more confident now, as though they'd seen the light at the end of the tunnel. "It's perfect, actually, I think. I figured you'd be really excited, but I did think it was only fair to tell you as soon as possible."

Sunlit gaped.

"You'd better just come out and tell her," said Joy. "Before she tests out her new railing."

"Good point." Taiwo grinned. "It's Chip. Chip and his father, Pa Daleson. They put in a really good application, and we're going to offer them the first chance to officially take in Fish. Starting as soon as tomorrow, if you'd all like."

"We all?" asked Sunlit, dazed.

"The sooner he can settle in somewhere permanently, the better, right?" said Taiwo.

"That *is* wonderful news," Joy said, meanwhile. "So sweet!"

"Yes, very sweet," said Sunlit, much more slowly.

"I know it's a bit abrupt. That's why I wanted to be the one to tell you," Taiwo said sympathetically. "We'd better get back to dinner now though. I wasn't kidding about the tacos being gone."

"Right." Sunlit followed her friends down the pier, one foot in front of the other. This had been the goal all along, right?

The pier was cleaned up, Joy was self-sufficient, and Fish had found a home. And yet—there was something lurking deep within Sunlit—she was uncomfortably aware of a distant problem headed her way, like the shadow of a kraken far beneath calm waves.

21

A Fated Decision

<blockquote>

While many may be inclined to dismiss the common clam as a mere metaphor for shyness or a dubious seafood treat, there is more to this mollusk than meets the eye. Clams are impressive filter feeders who often give clues about local water quality. That is why, if you encounter a sick clam, it would behoove you to check its environment carefully.

—*from* Traverse's Guide to Marine Vertebrates, Invertebrates, and Magical Outliers

</blockquote>

That strange, unsettled feeling at the back of her mind stayed with Sunlit as she went through her morning chores.

It certainly couldn't have been anxiety about her duties. As she had told Fish just days before, animal care is animal care, no matter if you're in a new facility or somewhere you've worked for years. It was already habit to let herself out the back door and carry her pail down the narrow steps to the baby moon rays waiting in the boat. The lion seal was so accustomed to her presence that it just flapped a lazy flipper at her from the prow before rolling over and going back to sleep. Joy, too, was curled up in the boat and snoring. All was as it should be.

And yet the entire time, Sunlit was making worried notes to herself:

Have Ige take the morning shift with the babies

If he can mind his manners

The lion seal will probably be fine to go soon

Maybe just one more dose of medicine to finish out the course

I wish it would try to at least pretend *it's wary of people*

Taiwo gave official word that the boat can stay here as part of the shop

But Joy . . . ?

Sunlit shoved that last thought aside and climbed back up to the shop, turning her attention to the tanks.

The tank where Spick and Spann had been was scrubbed clean—a bit of late-night tidying she'd done once everyone else had finally left. Fish had been exhausted. But for some reason, Sunlit hadn't been able to sleep.

She checked on the crab and Iggy the salamander—*both probably not going to leave, one because of his survival prospects, one because . . .* She raised an eyebrow at Iggy. Iggy turned a circle atop his rock and gave her a wide salamander grin. Sunlit sighed.

The clams, though—those, she could turn loose in good conscience. Even though the life guards had been vague about how long they'd had the clams, she knew for certain now that they'd been with her for four days. Plenty long enough for signs of a curse to emerge. All four still looked entirely normal.

Sunlit washed out her pail and piled the clams into it, lifting them gingerly from their tank. Then, glancing around the shop once more to make sure it was secure and quiet, she slipped out the side door and headed for the beach.

The rising sun cast long shadows off of the boardwalk and reflected from a bank of clouds out over the ocean. The sand was still moist and cool, though the air was already warm. Sunlit's gaze trailed over Beachy Bakes and the empty lifeguard stand. It was far too early for tourists, and therefore most of the townsfolk were still abed, too.

Perfect for clams, Sunlit thought to herself. She picked a spot near the pier and squatted down to set her charges free.

"Morning, Sunlit!"

Sunlit leapt upright, so shocked she nearly spilled her clams in every which direction. From the beach behind her, Sabrina tipped her hat with glimmering blue nails. "I know," she said. "It's weird seeing me in the morning, right? Normally I like the evening shift. But I'm covering for a friend and figured I'd check the beach. I'm sorry I missed the pier cleanup yesterday!"

"Oh," said Sunlit, her pulse slowly returning to normal. "That's alright. I'm sure all you police officers are very busy."

"We are and we aren't," Sabrina said easily. Then she added, "I suppose you know about all the mayhem over Fish. You'd be the best to know about it, after all. I will say, following up on all those complaints has definitely kept us busy lately."

"There have been that many complaints?" Sunlit blinked. She hadn't realized just how much Officer Ebb and Taiwo with their cheerfulness had been protecting her.

Sabrina shrugged. "Most are silly. No one who's met Fish takes it too seriously. Say, did he really fix your pipes that day?"

"He—he really did," Sunlit answered, dazed.

"Must be an interesting kind of magic," Sabrina said. But it didn't sound ominous coming from her. She smiled again as she said, "I'll leave you to it. Tell him hello for me when he gets up!"

As the police officer walked back up the beach, Sunlit watched, frozen. The bucket of clams was heavy in her hand. *An interesting kind of magic.* What a strange take on curses . . .

Could one person's "curse" be someone else's "interesting magic"? Sunlit shook her head. The question was better put to a student of magic theory, or philosophy. As a marine biologist, she did not feel up to the task.

And as she crouched down once more and tucked the first clam into a little tide pool, that amorphous dread swimming in her subconscious surfaced for a brief moment. *What if it really is cursed? Should I have kept them longer?*

But I can't really keep them longer, she tried to remind herself, watching the clam bubble happily in its new home. Her hand was still extended. Snatch it back? Or let it be?

I could tell Chip to bring by the local Witch to check for sure, Sunlit reasoned, *but I'm already asking him so much. And the Witch might not think it's worthwhile to bother with a couple of clams . . .*

. . . But if they are cursed, they could wreak havoc on the whole beach ecosystem . . .

Sunlit looked over her shoulder, at the pristine crescent of sand stretching away from her. *This is silly,* she told herself firmly. *They're not cursed. I'm not doing anything wrong. This is where they're supposed to be.*

Before that little bit of doubt raised its head once more, she quickly unloaded the next three clams. Like a criminal, she straightened up quickly and turned on her heel and—

—and nearly tripped over Fish. "Ahh!" Sunlit cried out automatically, then bit her lip.

"What are you doing?" Fish asked brightly.

"It was time to let the clams go back to the beach," she said, uneasy and trying her utmost to mask it. "We'd better get back to the shop. We have some cleaning up to do."

"Because I have to take my book and puzzle to Chip's house?" Fish guessed, reaching out for her hand.

Sunlit took his cool little hand in hers as they began to walk. "Yes, Fish, that's exactly it."

* * *

Last night, of course, Sunlit had told Chip—who had helped her tell Fish. So none of this was any surprise.

As Fish sat in the middle of the ocean rug, trying to stuff pieces of blue whale back into its box, Sunlit folded his tiny clothes. Biscuit watched them from one of the beams bracing the roof.

"*Any port,*" he squawked. "*Any port!*"

It was what he'd said the first night they stayed there. Sunlit wondered if the parrot saw them packing and understood that this would be their last.

Any port in a storm. When they'd first settled in to sleep in this attic, Sunlit had accepted it as a sort of desperate inevitability. But now . . . she told herself that packing up to leave was just an inevitable, but somehow it didn't feel fitting. And it certainly didn't feel like a relief. This wasn't how she'd imagined things at all.

"Sunlit," said Fish, as he tried his hardest to stuff a tail fin into the box, "what if the pieces don't go back together?"

"They will," she said, distracted.

"Maybe it's two whales now instead of one," said Fish.

"*Two whales!*" Biscuit agreed.

"Helloo up there," Joy called from the shop floor. "I've just been to get some breakfast. The urchins are very tasty today!"

Hearing her sent a pang through Sunlit's heart.

"Joy," Fish yelled back, "my one puzzle is two puzzles now!"

"Does that happen when you leave them alone too long?" Joy wondered.

"It doesn't," Sunlit insisted, a little exasperation showing. "I'm sure it's just one. Here, Fish, I'll pack that. You roll up your blanket. Joy, will you watch the shop for a bit while we're gone?"

"I could do with a little rest," Joy agreed amiably from below.

"Am I taking the blanket?" Fish clambered over his cot. "I thought we were supposed to give it all back."

"Oh." Sunlit had forgotten about that part—forgotten she'd said it out loud, at least. It was true she didn't need to take any of the things she'd borrowed from the emergency bank herself. She had more borrowed blankets and clothes and furniture, back in her aunt's otherwise empty house . . .

"I think they won't mind about this blanket," Sunlit decided. The townsfolk owed that much to Fish, at least.

"That's good," Fish declared. He was rolling atop his bundled up blanket like a hamster stuck on the outside of its wheel. "I like it because it makes me think of home. Do you think my puzzle is cursed, Sunlit? Is that why it's bigger now?"

Sunlit froze, torn between the words "home" and "cursed."

"Fish," she said finally, hoarsely, "you really shouldn't talk about curses."

"*Talk it out!*" squawked Biscuit, sounding rather irritable.

"Why shouldn't I? Are they bad?" Fish asked, innocently.

"They're . . . People think they're bad. Of course they are," Sunlit said. Sabrina and her *interesting magic* loomed in her mind, making her uncertain. "It's just not a very nice thing to talk about."

As Sunlit stuffed his clothes in a sack, Fish seemed to think this over. "Do you only talk about nice things?"

"*Curses!*" said Biscuit.

"Biz, hush," Sunlit said, exasperated. "I don't know, Fish, I . . . You're only really supposed to talk about nice things, yes."

"But what about lion seal snot?" Fish asked. "And spinach? And telling Biscuit to hush?"

Sunlit slowed her packing, amused at Fish's list of "not nice" topics despite herself. "Okay, maybe it's okay to talk about not nice things. Just not all the time."

"Is it because you don't want to think about sunburns?" Fish asked.

"No," Sunlit said. And yet—she did wonder. Was it possible that her own vulnerability made her more worried about Fish's potential vulnerabilities, too? Was that *fair?*

She set the thought aside for now. Now wasn't the time to ponder her navel; now was the time to pack up Fish and get him to the Dalesons' so that she could get the Sanctuary ready for a short absence.

For a minute—for just a brief second—returning to the University felt like the real curse.

"*Not nice, not nice,*" Biscuit called from the rafters.

Sunlit sighed. "I'm sorry, Fish, I'm just a little distracted today. Everything will turn out fine. Do you want anything for breakfast?"

The little boy smiled, all thought of curses forgotten. "Muffins!"

22

A Dark Horizon

. . . Indeed, with its gorgeous sunsets and hidden histories, its picturesque cliffs and fantastic tales, any discerning tourist will find that it is easy to fall in love with Seaside—and very difficult to leave it behind.

—*from* A Guide to Seaside (for the Discerning Tourist)

If Fish thought it was strange that they bought half a dozen muffins from Arietta without staying to chat, he said nothing. Fortunately, it had taken them so long to pack up that by the time they got to Beachy Bakes, the bakery was full of early risers. Sunlit hoped the crowd was a good excuse for her desire to dash in and out.

That looming feeling was only getting worse. At this point, she would hardly have been surprised to look over her shoulder and see a shark fin coming for her.

Her stomach was in knots and she couldn't have eaten a muffin if she tried, but she *was* able to find Chip's house. That rolled canvas map from the information booth still came in handy. They walked due south from the boardwalk, past the fishers' marina toward "Fisher's Village." Sunlit walked carefully, her nose in her map, but Fish was bouncing as he looked every which way.

And it was Fish who spotted it first, actually. They walked down the prim row of little cabins, each wooden home a different color, with decorated shutters and nets hanging in the scrubby yards. Pink, blue, yellow, green. Fish gave a happy yell and raced toward a lavender cabin with a bench out front.

Pa and Chip both were sitting on a bench beside the open front door. They rose, smiling, as Fish came to meet them. For a moment, Sunlit found she couldn't walk. She stood stock still, even forgot to breathe as she watched the little boy launch himself into the mens' arms.

This is where he's supposed to be, she reminded herself.

She knew it was true. There was true joy in the Dalesons' faces, and in Fish's excited movements—the kind of joy a certain giant otter had once accused Sunlit of not knowing much about. It made her happy to see it.

But it still didn't stop the anxiety dogging her steps . . .

Sunlit made it up to Chip just as Pa was taking Fish inside, giving him the "grand tour." Chip insisted on hugging Sunlit before she set Fish's bags and the box of muffins on the bench. Even with the weight out of her arms, her shoulders felt heavy.

"Listen," she said, quiet and urgent.

"Sure thing, Professor," said Chip, his smile wide enough to give Iggy the salamander a run for his money.

"I'm going back," Sunlit began.

Chip's ears twitched, a sign of mild surprise. "To the shop already? Don't you want to stay and help him settle in? I took the whole day off. Don't feel like you have to rush—"

"No, Chip," Sunlit interrupted, her words so suddenly forceful that her friend looked back at her in wide-eyed shock. "I need *you* to look after the shop. I'm going back to New West Key."

"What?" Chip reeled. "Me?"

"Just for a little while," Sunlit added, fast and low. "I'll sign it over to the university, and I'm sure they'll send someone out. It might even become a full-fledged outpost of the Marine Center—"

"But I have to fish," Chip protested. "It may not seem like it, but I *do* work, you know."

"Have Ige help with the morning shift," said Sunlit.

"Like Ige would do anything I told him to," Chip retorted.

Sunlit put her hands on her hips. "He would if you would actually *talk* to him!"

Chip shook his head. Glancing hastily into the house before lowering his voice, he said, "This is all ignoring the main point. You can't leave, Sunlit!"

"What do you mean I can't leave?" He'd used her name. She hadn't expected him to fight her on this. She felt like she was drowning.

"You can't leave," Chip repeated, hissing. "*You* belong here. Not some undergrad from some university on the other side of Beyond. *You're* the one who built this place."

"There's nothing wrong with undergrads," Sunlit argued, gasping for breath.

"I'm sure they're fine," Chip said, waving one hand in a gesture both apologetic and dismissive. "But they aren't *you.*

What's Joy have to say about this?"

"It's not Joy's decision," Sunlit replied. That shark fin following her had grown the arms of an octopus, and it was latched on to her back, its arms constricting her chest and making it difficult to speak. "I'm not her keeper. She's not mine. I came out because she needed help, and she's had it. She's going to be fine now. She'd basically fine already. And Fish has a home. So there's no reason for me to—"

"What did you say?" Fish poked his head out the door. "Sunlit, did you see my new house? It's really cool!"

"I will in a minute," Sunlit lied desperately.

"Pa said he saw a sailfish," said Fish. "*I'm* a sailfish!"

"That's really cool," Sunlit said, flailing.

"Are we going to eat the muffins?" Fish asked, spying the box on the bench.

"Sure thing, buddy," Chip broke in. "Will you take them into the kitchen and get some plates? The Professor here was just telling me about how to take care of the marine shop."

Fish paused, box of muffins in his hands, looking up at Chip. "Are you going to work there now too? I work there."

"Good," Chip said. "You can show me all about it."

"Sunlit can show you all about it," Fish said, his cheer slowly shifting into suspicion. He turned to look up at her with his head on one side. "Aren't you going to still work there too?"

"Not—not exactly," Sunlit said.

For a very long moment, Fish held her gaze. His wide, dark eyes were inscrutable. Sunlit felt like a captain who had refused to go down with the ship.

But the ship was fine—it was going to be fine, if not better, without her. *She* was the one tethered to the bottom of the sea.

Fish turned very politely to Chip. "I like your house. I promise not to make it break in a big wave."

"I appreciate that, buddy," Chip said. He sounded sad and tired, but he rubbed Fish's head affectionately. "Even if you do, we'll just make a new one."

Fish nodded solemnly and retreated, box of muffins in tow.

"That kid loves you," Chip hissed to Sunlit, fluffy ears tucked back in distress. "*We* love you. Even *Ige* loves you. Stay."

"I can't," Sunlit said, fighting the lump in her throat. "I was never supposed to."

"I don't care about 'supposed to,'" Chip growled.

"Well, I *do*!"

Sunlit surprised even herself with her vehemence. She blinked, fighting the impulse to look around, searching for who had spoken. Had that really been her?

But of course it had. She'd built her whole life around *supposed to*. Helping the Marine Center, the other students, her professor. Helping her grandparents, her aunt, even when they no longer needed her. Helping the animals and downplaying the fact that she had inexplicable intuitions about them. Doing everything she could, literally spending her own savings, to rescue an otter in distress . . .

. . . And now returning to New West Key, as she'd told her professor she'd do. What reason was there to do otherwise? Why was this so difficult?

"Fine," Chip said hoarsely. "But I warn you right now, I can only spare three days to fill in for you. Tops. And the moment Ige tries to tell me what to do, I'm out of there. I don't care *how* many baby moon seals or whatever you have there."

"I released the clams this morning, and I'll probably let the lion seal go later. There's really not that much," Sunlit said, the tears sneaking down her cheeks. "I'm sure the university will send someone soon, at the very least to check it out. It's just however long the paperwork takes for me to donate it, is all."

"Stay until the paperwork goes through," Chip said, pouncing on this opening. "It's got to be easier to do it if you're here, right? Won't you need Taiwo's approval and everything? And Rachel over at the bookstore can help—"

"I'm going to the town council next." Sunlit ignored the suggestion of the bookshop, drawing her long-sleeved shirt tighter around her body. She couldn't tell if she was freezing or if she was in shock. But why should she be in shock? She'd known all along this time would come. "It's really best if I go. Oh, Chip, I really owe you, I—I know I—"

"Come on," he said, softening the moment her resolve broke. He spread his arms wide, and Sunlit fell forward into them, not even remembering that she ought to wrap her own arms around him too. Instead she stood in his embrace, swaddled up like an anemone that's just had the fright of its life. Chip rested his head on her shoulder. "I wouldn't *actually* abandon the baby moon things," he mumbled. "But you know how irritating Ige gets. Couldn't you ask someone else to fill in? Arietta? One of the lifeguards?"

"Chip," said Sunlit, distracted, "is it windy? Or is it just me not being able to catch my breath?"

"The storm's been coming in for hours," Chip said with a huff. "Everyone but a landlubber like you would know that."

Sunlit didn't bother arguing about New West Key being *also* on the ocean, and her heritage being perfectly seafaring. She did wonder if the storm would get in the way of her closing up the shop. It seemed like it might be a big one. The world, she realized, was even darker than it had been at dawn. And still, there was that awful feeling of something about to breach . . .

"There you are," said Pa, poking his head out the door. And then, "Isn't Fish out here playing with you?"

23

A Sudden Strike

> *Every hospital must have storm preparedness procedures in place. An evacuation plan and good communication is critical. Even with state-of-the-art spells and magitech devices, the forces of nature are not to be dismissed. Particularly not when lives are at stake . . .*
>
> *—from* Standard Practices for a Safe & Sanitary Animal Medic

Almost without talking about it, Sunlit and Chip were in action.

Fish was nowhere to be found—not in the cozy cabin nor in its attic nor in the little yard behind it. The muffins were in the kitchen, and Fish had vanished, leaving only one trace: a small puddle on the tiled kitchen floor. There was no sign of him on the road, either.

Where could he have gone in only a minute? Sunlit had no answer. It seemed like she might turn and trip over him—and at the same time, it felt like he might be anywhere. The wind had picked up, and all her other plans were forgotten.

Pa stayed behind to watch the house, just in case Fish returned there. Chip went through the neighborhood and nearby roads before heading for the marina. And Sunlit went straight back to Marine Sanctuary.

The first raindrops pelted her face as she yanked open the front door.

Joy, curled up behind the register like a cat in a basket with her head on the counter, perked up immediately. "Back so soon?"

"Joy," Sunlit was already gasping, "have you seen Fish? Did he come back here?"

"Fish is lost?" Joy's whiskers twitched furiously. "I haven't seen him since you left. This is terrible. What if someone sees him do magic?"

"We'll find him, we're going to—" Sunlit lost her words. Joy's abrupt and uncharacteristic worry had activated her habit of being reassuring and calm, but this situation was too much for habits. And Joy had just introduced a new layer of tension. "Everyone already knows anyway!"

"That doesn't mean they'll react well if they see proof," said Joy, sitting up on her front paws.

"At this point, it's already raining too hard to see much of—"

Sunlit paused again. She'd turned around, gesturing at the open door and the storm behind her. But then a new thought struck. "Do you think it *is* Fish?"

"The doorway?" Joy's wide brown eyes were inscrutable.

"The *storm!*" Sunlit was so wound up she could have stamped her foot. "The storm! He heard me talking to Chip. I couldn't *lie* to him. Maybe he thought the whole Sanctuary is going away, or that—or that—"

"You have to go and find him," said Joy, more to the point.

"You stay here in case he comes back," Sunlit agreed. "I'm going down the boardwalk. If Chip comes by, tell him I'm trying Arietta's first!

"And make sure Biscuit stays inside," she directed, halfway out the door.

"And oh," Sunlit added, poking her head back in, "if the storm gets too bad, you might bring in the lion seal and the baby moon rays!"

She dashed out again without thinking *how* Joy might accomplish such a thing, because when it came to emergencies, Sunlit didn't think much about *how*. She just thought about *need*.

Her own needs of course were ignored as she slipped on the wet boardwalk and ripped the knee of her overalls. Her hat had long since been lost. The rain plastered her short hair to her head. She hadn't been this cold at least since her last day at the Marine Center, where air conditioning spells were common (in Seaside, the townsfolk were apparently resigned to being hot).

Needless to say, when Sunlit arrived at the bakery door, Arietta already knew something was wrong.

"Come in at once," the little gnome demanded, shutting the door behind Sunlit. "I was just about to lock up. Whatever it is, you have excellent timing."

"I have terrible timing." Sunlit could have cried as she glanced around the empty, darkened shop. "Fish isn't here? You haven't seen Fish?"

Arietta's hand flew to her mouth as her eyes widened. "No, I haven't. My goodness, is the poor boy missing? In *this* storm? They say it might be worse than the last one!"

"I'm worried he's helping it. Or caused it. I don't know, I

don't have any idea how his magic works," Sunlit despaired. Thinking that this storm might be worse than the one that injured Joy's tail and ripped up half her pier was not helping any. Now, she echoed Joy's worry. "What if someone like Coral found him?"

"Coral?" Arietta blinked. "Oh, no, did she say something to him?"

"Not to him. I don't think so. I guess I'm not sure." Sunlit wrung her hands and realized absently that she was dripping all over Arietta's clean tile floor. "I better go out and keep looking. Thank you, Arietta. Will you—would you—if you were planning to stay here—"

"I'll keep an eye out in case he comes by," Arietta promised.

"Thank you." Sunlit's relief was intense, but brief. "I have to go."

"Of course you do. And come back here afterward for warm tea and food!" Arietta called, as she saw her out the door.

The wind was raging now. Sunlit could hear the bakery door clanging and snapping behind her. Every nearby window was shuttered, all the booths buttoned down. There was no one on the boardwalk—no one, except two shadowy figures standing out by the rail.

Sunlit made straight for them, as though she'd been an extrovert all her life. She began calling out to them before she even recognized the forms. The wind tore away her voice. When they finally turned around, hearing her shouts, she saw Taiwo's bright eyes and the solemn face of Officer Ebb.

"Please," Sunlit heard herself say, faintly against the storm.

"You shouldn't be out here." Because his back was to the ocean, his words racing in the same direction as the wind, Officer Ebb's voice came across as much more firm.

"We've only just gotten everyone off the beach," Taiwo added helpfully. "You should make sure your shop is safe. The weather station up the coast sent out a warning. This storm came practically out of nowhere."

"No," Sunlit protested, trying to find her breath. "I'm looking for Fish. Have you seen him? Wasn't he on the beach?"

"Fish is missing?" Officer Ebb stood up straight. "For how long?"

"He's gone out into the storm?" Taiwo sounded doubtful. Over their shoulder, the waves crashed in huge white sprays of foam.

"Not that long," Sunlit panted. She had no concept of time in this state. "Just when the storm was starting."

Officer Ebb's eyes on hers were sharp. "You don't think . . . ?"

"Fish would never," said Sunlit, outraged. Even though most everyone, Fish included, thought that he *had*.

"I agree with Sunlit," said Taiwo stoutly. "Fish would never. Look at this storm. It's too much for a child."

Wiping water from her eyes, Sunlit could see that Officer Ebb looked like he might argue. But instead, he stuck to the matter at hand. "No adult should be out in this weather, let alone a child. If he's outside, he'll be wanting to go inside. Have you checked the likely places?"

"Chip's house, my shop, Arietta's," Sunlit said without thinking about it. "I can't think of anywhere else. I can't think . . ."

"You might have just missed him," Taiwo pointed out. "Is there someone at each place waiting?"

Sunlit nodded, still wiping at her face. Down the boardwalk, a trash can tumped over and began to roll away.

"We'll check with them again," Officer Ebb decided. "And if he hasn't turned up yet, I'll have my officers search."

"Wait!" Sunlit protested. "What if—what if an officer finds him and—what if he doesn't like them?"

This was met with stares and an uncomfortable pause that had no chance at silence, thanks to the storm. Officer Ebb's poker face was very good. Either he had no idea what she *actually* meant, or he was determined to ignore it. Taiwo's large eyes were more sympathetic, and Sunlit thought they could understand—it wasn't that Fish would take some kind of petty dislike to a stranger in such a circumstance, but if that stranger approached him accusing him of bringing misfortune on the entire town . . .

"He's only just settled in," Sunlit added. Her voice was too weak to be heard over the rain.

But in that moment, a warm hand found her shoulder. The rain ceased to buffet her head. Chip was on one side, and Ige, holding a heavy-duty umbrella, was on the other.

"Found Ige checking on the Sanctuary as I came over from the marina," Chip explained to Sunlit, yelling with the practiced ease of a sailor against the storm. To Taiwo and Ebb, he added, "You've heard about our search?"

Our search. Sunlit's knees wobbled. She could have melted in gratitude.

But he is still out there . . .

"I'll search the surf," Ige shouted, his lifeguard's voice equally commanding against the noise.

"You will not!" Both Taiwo and Chip spoke in unison.

"I'll get word to Mother," Taiwo went on. "There's no need for anyone to swim out there right now. I'll also tell the council."

Don't tell them, Sunlit thought desperately, thinking of cold Clementina. But at the same time, Seaside and its waters were too big for her to search alone. She needed the help. She just had to trust that they wouldn't think the worst of Fish.

"I'll get the Witch on hand," Officer Ebb decided. "However you feel about it, Haven, magic will be a quicker search than officers. So that's your best choice."

"Yes, okay," Sunlit nodded, strengthened by the tiny patch of calm Ige and Chip had created between them. "Do it. Please."

"I'm going to loop back and check on Pa," Chip shouted. "Maybe Fish went back to the house."

"I'm going with you," Ige shouted across Sunlit. "We can check the town if we need to."

For once, there was no argument.

Sunlit spoke up. "I'm just going to check the beach really quick. Then I'll check the annex and the pier."

"And stay there," Officer Ebb shouted. "We need to be able to find you with news."

"But I couldn't—" Sunlit gaped.

"I agree," Ige yelled. "Fish would look for you there."

"But—but—"

"For once, my brother is right," Taiwo added.

Sunlit looked to Chip, pleading.

He shook his head. "Much as it pains me, I think they're right, Professor," he said hoarsely. "Plus, your animals will need you, too."

"Fine!" Sunlit didn't mean it to sound petulant and final, but the word was flung out with force.

Still, Taiwo smiled at her grimly. "Good. Then we can all meet back at the Sanctuary."

"No more time to waste, now," Officer Ebb agreed. The two

began walking, pushed along by the wind as they headed for town.

Chip squeezed her shoulder before he and Ige, too, took off. Watching them go, Sunlit saw Ige tug Chip under the cover of his umbrella.

And now it was just her—her, and the beach, and the storm. Sunlit glanced up and down the boardwalk one more time. Rain was running in streams and waterfalls off the shop roofs. The ocean roared, so close it drowned out her very thoughts. The beach was gray and cloudy, devoid of life, an elemental playground . . .

But something—some spark within her—some feeling— tugged her toward the sand.

24

A Pouring Rain

> *Nobody's seen a storm dragon in a really long time. Some people think they live on an island far out at sea. There, they can play in the waves and make whirlpools of wind. And out on the open water, the storms won't hurt anyone!*
> —*from* Children's Encyclopedia of Deep Sea Creatures

The storm wasn't wind and rain any more—it was waves flying through the air, like the ocean was doing its best to take back the town. The old pier, the bait shop, even the new marina beyond, they were only pitch-black shadows in the foam-flecked chaos. So far, though, they were holding fast.

Sunlit ran down onto the sand, following her instinct. The water had risen to the highest tide levels, the largest waves licking at the lifeguard stand. Everything there was tied down and solid. The beach had been left to the ocean. Did she really expect to find anything?

She didn't expect, but she still had that feeling. She turned and looked over her shoulder, peering under the boardwalk even. The shadows there were nearly inscrutable. Frustrated, she ran down the beach toward the shop, shouting now as she went. Her shouts were lost in the wind.

But she kept looking, her certainty rising. Somehow, she knew, she was close to finding something; even amid all this wildness and darkness. If she just kept looking . . .

There, in the darkest shadow, underneath the old pier, where Sunlit had just recently released a group of clams, was a curled little figure. She could only see it by squinting hard against the rain.

Fish.

Sunlit ran across the beach to him, but she had to pause often, to catch her breath and to dodge the waves. Some were strong enough to knock her over, and getting bigger. She kept her eyes trained on him, on the pier, but it was impossible to run there in a straight line. She tripped over driftwood in the sand and a wave rolled over her elbows and knees. When she regained her balance and refocused on Fish, she could see now that he was glowing.

But it wasn't a wild, powerful, crackling, calling-down-storms and destroying-piers-with-ocean-magic glow . . .

. . . It was a thin, desperate glow, like mist in a tornado, rising from him and being whipped away into the storm. It was little. It was *something*—Fish himself was something, some kind of magic—but Sunlit knew in her bones that it was not the cause of the storm.

The *feeling* was back.

She charged straight through the next wave and had him in

her arms without another thought. He'd been clinging to the columns under the pier, his magic just enough to divert the waves around himself. What had been a little tide pool earlier that morning was now a little whirlpool, a safe hiding place just for a very distressed Fish.

"We're in it together," Sunlit said, gritting her teeth against the storm's howl, uncertain if Fish could hear her. "I've got you."

And she did. She held him very securely against her chest, but she knew instinctively not to run back out into the storm. It would only take one rogue wave to separate them. Better, she decided, to stay here, and to trust in Fish's magical safe spot until the waves died down.

After a moment, Fish let go of the column and wriggled in her grasp. He turned to clasp his arms around her neck.

"I don't want you to go," he said, his wet head at her ear. "I don't want you to ever go."

Sunlit opened her mouth and closed it, with only a mouthful of saltwater to show for her effort. She certainly wasn't going to leave Fish in a storm. But was she going to leave him in Seaside?

"I'm sorry," Fish added, burying his flat nose in her neck. "I made the storm. It's my fault."

"I was going to say the same thing to you," Sunlit told him, turning her head to shield them both as the spray off the top of a wave whisked around them. "I thought it was my fault. I made you sad."

"You didn't do it on purpose," said Fish. "I forgive you."

Sunlit's eyes opened wide—and then she squeezed them shut. "Fish, sweetheart. You didn't do it on purpose either. The storm is not your fault. None of the storms have been your fault."

For a moment, she wasn't sure if he had heard her over the roar of the wind.

Then he said so quietly she barely caught it, "Do you still like me if you know?"

In the darkness, the words made perfect sense to Sunlit.

She saw all their time in Seaside with perfect clarity. Somewhere deep inside, Fish had known all along that he wasn't the one who had destroyed the pier. But he had accepted that responsibility as a way to make himself relevant to her, to Ige and Chip, to everyone in Seaside. Even if it wasn't a good thing, it was something he could talk to them about.

Do you still like me if you know?

Sunlit could hear the words echoing in her own mind, repeating and expanding. *Could they still like me if they knew I wasn't an expert, a "Professor?" Could they still like me if I didn't know the right thing to do—and make sure I did it? Could they still like me even if I had no excuse to be here, no obvious way to fit in?*

Could they still like me if I wasn't of use?

This was the shadow, the sea monster that had been stalking her all day. All her life. This was the true curse. And now it had swallowed them both.

Sunlit held on to the little boy with all her might. "Fish, I like you so much. I think you're really cool. I *love* you, Fish. Nothing can ever change that. And you don't have to do anything, or *not* do anything, in order for me to love you. I just *do*."

"I love you, too," Fish snuffled. "Even if you go away."

"Thanks," Sunlit said, smiling despite herself.

"Even if you're not always smart."

"Point taken," she replied, wryly. "But I don't have to be smart to know that everything's going to turn out okay, one way or another, right?"

"Right," Fish agreed, with another sniff.

"Okay, then." Sunlit laid her head against his. "We're just going to wait this out. Not too much longer now. Want to bet?"

Fish tightened his arms around her neck. He didn't want to bet, apparently. But it felt good just to hold him in their little magic haven while the storm wore itself out.

* * *

It was Ige and Chip who found them.

Sunlit had no idea how long it took. But the storm *did* start to ease. And as it did, the waves came more softly, rolling around her knees rather than leaping for their throats. But Fish's little magic cocoon of water-repelling stayed up. As light hit that faint glowing mist that Fish gave off, it refracted into the smallest, gentlest little pieces of rainbow Sunlit had ever seen.

Through this beautiful haze, two forms barreled down the beach toward them.

"*There* you are!" cried Chip.

"Why didn't you come out as soon as you could?" Ige shouted.

Sunlit took a moment to focus. At the sound of their voices, Fish's magic had abruptly winked out. Now it was just her, standing knee-deep in sand and soaked to the bone, holding up a normal—if mysterious—little boy.

She decided not to try to explain everything. Seeing the results of Fish's magic had been unlike anything she could describe. It felt like watching a hole within herself fill up with crystalline light.

"We've been looking everywhere. The Witch said you had

206

to be at the bait shop but you weren't there," Chip said, as he collided with them both. He was just as wet as they were, and crying, on top of that. Fish immediately shifted to return the three-way hug.

"We love you," he said.

"Good. I was just trying to tell the Professor here the same thing this morning," Chip said. He hoisted Fish into his arms, adding, "I love you too, kid. You have no idea."

"So no more running off into storms," Ige said sternly, as he helped Sunlit extract herself from the sand.

"Lay off," Chip retorted, his relief clearly giving way to revived cheer.

"I won't," Fish promised. From his perch in the crook of Chip's elbow, he reached for Ige. "I love you."

Ige hesitated, making sure Sunlit was free, and glaring at Chip, before finally heaving a sigh that shook his shoulders. "I love you, too. Even though you're all the worst," he declared, sweeping Sunlit and Fish into a hug that even included Chip. "Except you," he added to Fish.

"Now it's Sunlit's turn," Fish declared, delighted.

"I . . ." Sunlit swallowed, and realized that for the second time that day, she was choking back tears. "I can at least promise not to run away. If I *do* have to leave, I'll make sure I tell you all proper goodbyes first. And . . . I'll still come back and visit."

"What do you mean, 'have to leave'?" Ige demanded, leaning back. "You own the pier. No one can tell you to leave."

"Thank you," said Chip, emphatically. "That's what I was trying to tell her!"

"Yes but . . . I do have duties back at the university . . ."

"We just had the storm of the century here," Ige informed

her, dark eyes glittering.

Sunlit gaped. "What do you . . . Is—is Joy okay?"

"Everyone's fine," Chip assured her. "It's a good thing we managed to clean up the pier in time. But what he *means* is, if the last storm turned up a handful of injured animals, imagine how many more will be turning up now!"

Fish caught on now, too. "You could fix them, Sunlit!"

"And the town would pay," Ige added, looking rather smug. "The other lifeguards and I've been working on our contacts at town council, and now they'll *have* to help support the shop."

"How could they say no?" Chip agreed.

"You—you've been trying to get Taiwo and the others to pay for the shop?" Sunlit asked, disbelieving.

"In fairness to Taiwo," said Ige, with all the begrudging respect of a sibling, "they *always* were in favor of paying the shop to take on animals found on the beach. They just had to work out how it would fit into the town budget."

"So now you have both duties and means to stay," Chip summarized. "Not that you needed either of them, of course. We'd let her sleep in our attic, wouldn't we, Fish?"

"When were you going to tell me?" Sunlit demanded of Ige.

"I assumed I was going to have time as soon as the storm blew over," he retorted. "Until *someone* told me you were planning to sneak off."

"I wasn't sneaking!" she protested.

"Poor Sunlit," said Fish. "Were you worried? You could stay with us. We'll sell sunscreen and buy muffins!"

"And keep clams in buckets," Chip agreed, nuzzling Fish until the little boy giggled.

"And do the town a service," Ige reminded them all. "So? What do you say?"

"I say . . ." Sunlit glanced from face to face, and finally smiled, truly, fully. "I say let's talk about it again once we're all clean and dry and finally getting a bite of breakfast."

<h1 style="text-align:center">25</h1>

<h1 style="text-align:center">A New Promise</h1>

> *I don't think I ever would have made it through those rapids without such a crew. A good friend by your side is worth all the fancy luggage and travel insurance magic can get you. Give me a solid companion, someone who can tell me my faults and see me through anyway, over a heap of charms or gold any day.*
> *—from I'm An Adventurer Here Myself*

It wasn't breakfast, but a late lunch that the friends convened over. Rain still pounded on the bait shop roof, but the wind had shifted away from town. Arietta had seen them on the boardwalk and run over with a basket brimming with pastries and thermoses of tea, creating such an inviting indoors picnic that Taiwo and Ebb elected to stay when they stopped by to check in.

And on top of that, Joy *had* managed to bring inside two

halves of a massive barrel full of rays, and a rather curious lion seal.

They layered blankets on the hard wood floor to make up for the lack of chairs or couches. The basket and all its scattered, unpacked contents took up the middle, while the friends settled round it—Ige and Chip beside each other, Sunlit noticed. At some point in the drama, they must have convinced Pa to come down to the shop too, for he sat in a corner on the one stool. Joy curled round it, chattering to him cheerfully about barrels and boats.

Fish was the true celebrity of the hour, though. He sat at the head of the blanket, between Sunlit and Chip. People kept reaching out to touch him, perhaps half unbelieving he had been found; but he didn't seem to mind. Even Biscuit flew down from his perch atop the fish tanks to butt Fish's head and steal some crumbs.

After the first round of sandwiches had been finished, Joy caught Sunlit's eye and motioned to the sales counter with her nose.

Sunlit made her way over, leaving Fish, Chip, and Ige in a serious discussion about what exactly made the best muffin. Joy dove behind the counter, so Sunlit went back there too, joining Joy at the back door. By cracking it open just enough, they could see the waves and rain still outside. So far, the pier and the annex were safe.

"Thank you so much for actually bringing in the lion seal and ray babies," Sunlit said, as the storm outside reminded her that Joy must have had some difficulty with the task.

"Funny to think that they and I were safe up here, while you and Fish were just down there, isn't it?" Joy glanced sideways out the door, her nose pointing down below the old pier.

"I guess so," said Sunlit uneasily. She lowered her voice, though between the storm and the chatter of their friends, there wasn't much chance of being overheard. "Are you upset I didn't try to call for you? I was just so focused—and the waves were so loud—it was hard enough just for me to find him—"

"Magic, some might say." Joy tugged the door shut with one paw, looking up into Sunlit's face placidly.

"Well . . ." Sunlit swallowed. She'd never discussed her *feelings* with Joy before. In fact, she'd not told anyone in Seaside. What was there to say? "Some might."

Joy remained in the nook behind the sales counter, effectively trapping Sunlit with her long body and tail. "But not the kind of magic that could also alert others?"

"Uh . . ."

"It's like this, kit," said Joy, settling in. "I know what it's like to be trapped—especially to be trapped right next to people who might be able to help, but can't. I know what it's like to be scared. But I also know how important it is to raise your voice."

Sunlit glanced around the shop, tugging at her sleeves. "But, Joy . . ."

"Don't 'but Joy' me," said the otter, firmly.

"But Joy," Sunlit repeated, emboldened as a thought came to her, "you were pretty out of it too, during the first storm. I'm sure you weren't thinking too clearly either—"

"And just who," said Joy, with great dignity, "do you think told young Chip to contact New West Key?"

Sunlit's jaw nearly hit the floor. "You didn't—he said—I thought—"

"I'm sure he wouldn't say anything other than the truth," Joy observed, "which is that he floated up below the pier that morning because he heard me yelling. And when he yelled back at me, I told him to contact the Marine Center at New West Key. I wasn't about to take my chances with a small town vet. No offense to rural animal care, of course, but when you are as . . . *unusual* as I am, you know what your options are, because they're limited."

"*You?*"

"Me."

"Joy," said Sunlit, slowly, "where are you from again?"

"I don't dwell on the past, kit," said Joy airily. "Do you see my point now?"

Sunlit's mind was still boggled. "Um . . ."

"Look at all these people here," Joy demanded. "Did you need to go down to, and stay under, that pier all alone?"

"But—I—there wasn't time, and—Joy," Sunlit protested, finally martialling her thoughts, "you can't blame people for their response to stressful—"

"I'm not blaming you. I'm giving you the chance to learn and do better next time," Joy informed her. "Getting trapped like that gives you a lot of time to think things over, and it can be a good teaching experience. So, what did you learn?"

"What did I . . ." Sunlit glanced back at everyone, still eating and celebrating, and then at the determined otter before her. "I'll admit, I . . . It did make me think."

"And?"

"Why did you say it was magic?" Sunlit asked abruptly. "Finding Fish, I mean."

"Because both of you smell like it," Joy answered matter-of-factly. "It's a sort of tingly-on-the-nose sensation."

"Just today? After what happened?"

"No. Always."

"So you always knew . . ." *You've known all along something I don't,* Sunlit thought but didn't have the courage to say. *About Fish, and about me.*

"I'm not saying either one of you is a great mage, now," Joy went on amiably. "I've smelled my fair share of wondrous magic. With the two of you, it's a more ordinary, every day sort. That's how I knew you'd be the right one to take care of me."

"You couldn't have just swum away," Sunlit murmured, a little rebelliously.

"Not without trouble," said Joy easily. "But we always have choices, kit."

Joy's large dark eyes were fixed on Sunlit's meaningfully, and Sunlit sighed. "I know what you want me to say, Joy. I know I should be totally changed and should take Ige and Taiwo up on their offer and be very glad and promise everyone to be a good friend and . . . Well, I know that's how it would go in a disaster story. Person has a brush with loss and death, person turns their life around. But I'm not like that, Joy. I don't just *do* things like that. Not so fast."

"You don't, because you let yourself stay wrapped up in worries instead," Joy commented.

"Maybe, but—" Sunlit shrugged, a smile half-weary and half-knowing on her lips. "Come on, do you really want me to say that somehow I'll call you next time, and we'll *all* be dragged out into the storm? Wouldn't you rather just be healed and leave Seaside and go on with your own life?"

"Say something so disrespectful to me again and I will knock you out into the annex," Joy retorted. "It *is* my own life, and I'm already doing exactly what I want with it, thank you very much. You may know what infected tails and phlegmy coughs need, but you don't know what my heart needs. I don't need you worrying about me in order to get along. I need community, and I'm offering you a chance to own your place in it.

"And so is everyone here," Joy added, when an amazed Sunlit tried to distract herself by looking back at the ongoing feast. "They know that the point of life is not to *get through it alone*, like it's a marathon and someone's going to hand you a prize fish at the end. The point is to lift each other up. And if you can't let others lift you, then aren't you really just trying to pretend you're alone?"

Sunlit hugged her arms tight around herself—and then, on sudden impulse, unwrapped her protective embrace and hugged Joy instead. The otter's fur was warm and smelled like rain and salt and the cleaning potions they'd used on the shop floor.

If I could distill Seaside down into a candle, that's it, Sunlit thought, smiling despite herself as she buried her face in Joy's neck. *That, and marionberry muffins, and an undertone of "prize" fish.*

Joy wrapped Sunlit in one paw, tucking her head down over Sunlit's shoulder.

"I'll give it thought," Sunlit whispered. "I promise."

* * *

The next morning dawned cloudy and breezy, but otherwise quiet. While Joy went out to catch herself a shellfish breakfast, Sunlit and Biscuit paced around the Sanctuary, looking for storm damage.

While she was standing at the corner considering the ancient gutter with a despairing air, Sunlit noticed Chip and Fish walking over.

"Good morning," she called, surprised. Fish had seemed

perfectly content to go home with Chip and Pa the night before, so she had tried to act like it was normal, too. But she hadn't expected how nice it would feel to see him again, even after such a short time.

"We came to see the parade," Fish told her. "I'm an electric eel today! Electric eels like parades."

"I bet they would," said Sunlit, smiling. "But what parade?"

"You were saying yesterday how it was time to see the lion seal off," Chip explained, handing her a bit of toast, tomato, and egg wrapped up like a sandwich by way of saying hello. "I figured, you can't drag him out like you dragged him in. So we're all walking him down to the beach, then? Pa's coming by later with a couple more rope ladders he'd promised you. And his toolbox, he said."

"Hey, Joy is using the new pier!" Fish realized, as he spotted the otter clambering out of the water further down. He skipped off to meet her at the gate.

Sunlit took advantage of the convenient distraction. "You sure you weren't just coming over to make sure I'm still here? Also, you don't have to keep feeding me, you know."

"*I* know," said Chip, cheerfully. "But try telling that to Pa— and Arietta. I could barely eat breakfast after everything she made us stuff down yesterday."

"She did say she didn't want it all to go stale," Sunlit mused. It had made sense at the time, since the storm meant that surely no one would be buying baked goods that day, but now she wondered if it had just been a front. "But anyway, are you really here to see the lion seal off?"

"What? I can't care about the lion seal?" Chip teased, before becoming more serious. "I wanted Fish to see that it's not like he's giving something up. We can still be a part of life at the

Sanctuary. Right?"

"Right." *In fact*, thought Sunlit, *you might need to be—even if I stay. Or, especially if I stay?* "So . . . it wasn't because of me?"

"Not directly," Chip said, grinning.

"And it wasn't because you were hoping to see Ige doing his early-morning swim routine?"

"Lay off," Chip retorted. But he did laugh—and glance over Sunlit's shoulder to check the beach.

"Fish tells me it's time to release the lion seal," Joy announced as she came up to them, the little Fish in tow. "Marvelous day for it. The waters are a bit murky yet, but plenty of tasty morsels were stirred up by the waves last night."

"Well, in general, I don't think Chip and his promises about parades should dictate our release policy," Sunlit replied, amused despite herself. "But that said, we might not get a better time. It's definitely best to walk him out while the beach is quiet, anyway."

"I want to be at the front!" said Fish. His magic literally sparkled around him, giving an "electric eel" effect that was very festive. Sunlit smiled down at him and wondered how anyone could have ever thought his magic was harmful.

Of course, we still don't know what exactly he is or if he was cursed, Sunlit thought, as she opened the side door to check on the patient. *Maybe it never mattered anyway.*

The lion seal, which had sheltered inside with Joy overnight, was lingering in the corner by the door. It mewed at her hopefully as the morning light poured in. Sunlit gave it one last assessment, more confident in her judgment now than she had been while looking at the gutter: bright eyes, clean nose, even breathing, healthy fur. One impatient tail tapping at the wooden floor. Yes—the lion seal was ready to fend for itself again.

Her hand got caught in its mane as she helped guide it out the door. For that brief second, she got a feeling: one of adventure, excitement, and underlying gratitude.

She wiped at her eyes. Realizing that the animals knew what she was doing for them, and appreciated it, always made her teary.

Wait. I—I felt it?

Sunlit lifted her head, amazed at what had once been commonplace for her—in fact, what had once been an embarrassment, in the scientific hustle and bustle of the Marine Center. Here, it didn't seem so wrong.

In fact, here, it seemed perfect.

But in the time it took Sunlit to realize this, the parade had already begun. Fish led the way down from the boardwalk, while Joy and Chip flanked the lion seal, which moved awkwardly on dry land. Chip glanced back as if to say, *aren't you coming?*

Sunlit shut the door behind her and caught up with them just as a familiar lifeguard joined the retinue, too.

"What's this, some kind of party?" Ige asked, moving gracefully over the sand.

"We'll be out of your hair in a minute," said Chip, most likely *because* Ige had no hair to speak of. "Don't you dare tell us we should have had a permit."

Ige focused on Sunlit, refusing to rise to the bait. "Are you sure it's safe?"

"Positive," Sunlit said, revisiting her earlier feeling as she watched the lion seal flop along ahead of them. "That is, if you mean, is the lion seal safe to be out. If you're asking about storm damage or the beach or something . . ."

"All that's *his* job," Chip said, turning round to wink at her.

"Better leave him to it."

"Some of us do have important work to do," Ige grunted. "And today's going to be a long day."

Sunlit spared a glance over her shoulder, at the boardwalk. Though nowhere was as messy or ripped up as her pier had been, a few carts had been knocked down. She could see that water was still streaming down from every drain, cutting deep pathways through the sand to the ocean. Most of the shop windows were still dark. The beach around them was crowded with driftwood, buoys, seaweed, and debris. *Gifts from the sea,* as Pa might say. Or, in other words, junk.

"Just routine cleanup, mostly," Ige observed, glancing around with her. "It was a bad storm, but this is usually how bad storms go. We don't often get one that causes serious damage."

"Like the one that trapped Joy, you mean? Sunlit considered the otter, walking ahead in line like she couldn't hear them. For just a brief moment, she wondered if somehow Joy had set *all* of it up. But then she shook the thought away.

"I've been telling Taiwo for years it was bound to happen to that old pier sooner or later," Ige agreed. "Protection spells only go so far. They need someone actually looking after the place to work."

"Oh, are you an expert in magic now?" Chip called over his shoulder.

"I'm an expert on this beach," Ige growled back.

Sunlit was saved the effort of wading into this debate by a quirk of timing. They'd reached the waves.

Still at the head of the parade, with his feet ankle deep in the water, Fish turned back to look at Sunlit. "What now?"

"Watch out," Sunlit called back, laughing. The lion seal

flapped its tail and roared triumphantly as it reached the wet sand. Then, with a few last hops and a joyful swish of its mane, it dove headlong into an incoming wave and was gone.

"Just like that?" Fish asked, eyes shining bright.

"Just like that," Chip agreed, resting his hand on the little boy's head.

Ige looked on, smiling faintly. Joy turned back to nudge Sunlit, who looked back up the beach, towards the Sanctuary.

Already, she saw someone knocking at the closed door. Someone with a dripping bundle in their arms . . .

And her decision was made. Just like that.

26

A Cleansed Curse

Above all, it is imperative that the competent animal medic have confidence in themselves. To make the occasional mistake or miscalculation is natural. We are a part of the world, just like the creatures we treat. But if one is to be truly effective, one must know when to stand tall and choose without doubting oneself.
—*from* Standard Practices for a Safe & Sanitary Animal Medic

Several days later, Sunlit woke to Biscuit imitating an alarm clock. She looked up at the old wooden ceiling above her, and smiled.

There was so much to do. She rose and made her way to her little bathroom, her feet cushioned by an azure ocean rug. On the way, she passed a secondhand bureau filled with scrubs and long shirts and overalls—her entire wardrobe, in fact, had been delivered from New West Key the previous evening.

What had once been her kitchenette corner was now a comfy space with pillows and chairs, and a table for puzzles. There was even a new shelf with a few reference tomes and a stack of freshly borrowed books from the town bookshop. And what a few days before had been Fish's side of the room was now a little kitchen with another set of cabinets and a magitech kettle perfect for brewing tea. Near the ladder to the shop floor, Pa had even hung up hooks to hold a variety of wide-brimmed hats along the wall.

Biscuit flew down as Sunlit approached the hatch to go downstairs, nimbly avoiding the strings of parrot toys and perches which now hung from the rafters. Together, they landed in Marine Sanctuary.

Sunlit glanced over the stacks of fish tanks first. All was well: the crab that would never be quite well enough to go out, and Iggy the salamander who never seemed to want to. They had another tank of stressed fish staying with them, family friends of Spick and Spann, in a special tank Sunlit had privately dubbed the "house fish resort." There was also the old saturn snail, a slow healer indeed, his ring of sand slowly rotating around his shell. The ring was bigger these days, and Sunlit was certain that he would be right as rain in time. In the tank beside him, there were several hermit crabs that had been found amongst the storm debris. They'd immediately given Sunlit a sense for their names: Clotho, Lachesis, and Atropos, otherwise known as the three Fates of ancient myth. Grand names for little crabs, of course, but Sunlit thought they suited them. In the next tank, an anemone damaged by the surging waves was convalescing. Anemones could be very difficult to treat, and Sunlit considered herself lucky she'd been able to help this one. In one tank in the corner, a tiny, glowing fish circled, its magic still unknown. But in this case, the unknown magic was no threat—only a promise of something more to come.

Along the back wall, what had been Joy's corner now hosted a stout table and a set of shelves, also courtesy of Pa. Sunlit had lined up her tools and the potions and gauze from the university there. She had finally heard back from Professor McAlpin the day before—just a brief note, but it made Sunlit smile to think of it now, rather than filling her with frustration. Her professor had been vague but encouraging, and had promised more supplies soon. Sunlit would certainly have a use for them. Several old, damaged surfboards lined up together formed a screen to shelter the new exam room from the rest of the shop without cutting it off entirely.

Reaching under the counter into the icebox, Sunlit pulled out a bucket of ray food and a little extra tray besides. She went out the back door, Biscuit soaring gleefully above her. Several steps down in the annex, Joy slumbered peacefully, the water lapping at her fur. Sunlit stepped carefully around the giant otter, already used to navigating the old boat's slippery deck in her heavy boots.

The barrels holding the baby rays were anchored securely to the back of the annex now, and just in time: the rays themselves were growing, soaring through their little home and creating ripples which would soon be waves. Sunlit fed them and then secured their screen. It wouldn't be too much longer before she'd be setting them free.

But in the meantime, there was another visitor to check on. Sunlit turned and peered down into the sheltered water of the annex, finally spotting the dark octopus in its favorite spot—the corner where the boat's deck and aft met. She tossed it some seafood from her tray, tidbits which it accepted with one snakey tentacle. It had been found among the storm debris, and like the house fish, it seemed to need a little quiet. Once it wanted to leave, Sunlit had no doubt that it would do so. One old wreck of a boat could hardly stop an octopus.

Her one remaining creature was a little more worrisome. This was a normal-sized otter, the one that had been brought to the shop just as they let the lion seal go. Its leg had got caught between boats in the marina, resulting in a broken bone. Sunlit had given it a splint, and now Joy was giving it plenty of mothering. It slept curled up between her paws.

As Sunlit approached this time, Joy lifted her head, her whiskers twitching.

"Good morning! We're starting to have quite the routine, aren't we? The selkie left in the night," she said, cheerful but quiet so as not to disturb the impossibly tiny (though really quite average) otter nestled in her fur.

Sunlit nodded. "I thought he might." In the aftermath of the second storm, Marine Sanctuary had hosted its most magical visitor yet—Joy, Fish, and Sunlit herself notwithstanding, of course. But the mythical seal-man had been very anxious, only talking in brief snatches, only staying long enough that his sealskin could recover from a bad scrape. She was a *little* sad to hear he'd left without saying goodbye, but she wasn't surprised in the least. Selkies were known to be quite skittish, in general, and old stories about their seal skins being stolen so they were stuck in human form seemed to explain why.

The selkie had also been the one new creature Sunlit hadn't gotten any *feelings* from. But, like Joy, he had been perfectly capable of telling her his name and details himself. He'd simply chosen not to.

"We'll be known for magic care as much as anything else," said Joy, rather proudly. She'd never once considered leaving. Instead, she'd created a role for herself as shop assistant and animal guard—not to mention friend and advisor. And Sunlit could admit now, to herself as well as to others, that she dearly needed all of the above.

"There's a lot of magic in the ocean, so maybe it's good if those creatures know they can come here," Sunlit mused, leaning back against the side of the boat to rest. "I'm not sure how great our track record is, though. I mean, I never did 'cure' Fish. That's if he *was* cursed."

"What do you think cures curses?" Joy asked, amusement in her dark eyes.

"*I've got a feeling,*" Biscuit squawked from the pier railing nearby.

Sunlit smiled. "I don't know. But as Biz points out, sometimes I have felt cursed myself."

Though these days, she added to herself with amusement, *maybe I'd be more inclined to say "interesting."*

"And what's helped *you?*" Joy asked, practical to the last.

From the boardwalk, there came a faint clattering and the muffled sound of voices. Fish's high voice was instantly recognizable, but Chip's bright tones and Ige's grumble were just as clear. Sunlit recalled that it was Chip's day off, and he'd promised Fish a ride in his boat . . . and if Sunlit had to guess, she'd say that Ige had decided to go along to supervise. She had a sneaking suspicion they were about to invite her to come, too. That or they just felt like visiting the Sanctuary they'd helped her to build.

"Everyone's settled in well," she said to Joy, "and it'll only take me a moment to feed the tanks. Besides, we made pretty good money selling the last of the sunscreen potions and water pouches yesterday. What do you say we plan to open late today? We could try out our new 'out of office' sign."

Rachel had insisted that every shop needed one, along with a sign for fees, a sign for hours, and other very useful things. Sunlit had been unable to disagree. Now, she was glad.

"I could use a stretch," Joy agreed, shifting gently to place the little otter in a bed fashioned out of another barrel. There it could continue resting until it needed food, which Sunlit would store nearby. "You had the protective spells renewed?"

"Yesterday while you were out with the selkie," Sunlit reminded her. "I figured, since everyone went to so much trouble to help me fix things up, and since we have more patients now, it was better to do it sooner than later. Officer Ebb helped to . . . make the introductions, and keep the peace, I guess you could say. It turned out fine anyway. The Witch wasn't *so* bad."

Joy chuckled. She'd never been as upset with the townsfolk as Sunlit had. But now that Fish was happily settled, everything Taiwo and Chip had told her was true—the town rumor mill had moved on to something else. All thoughts of a dangerous Fish were forgotten. So Sunlit was making an effort to let her ire stay in the past, too. With Joy's insistent support, naturally.

They could both hear pounding now at the Sanctuary door, as Fish and Chip and Ige looked for them. The racket reminded Sunlit that she needed to install some kind of bell or buzzer for visitors to use instead. There were still so many improvements she had in mind for the Marine Sanctuary, but after Seaside's second big spring storm had brought in a wave of new creatures, she'd realized a need to pace herself.

And on that note, a day out in a boat with her friends sounded *wonderful.* But Sunlit hesitated. She looked up at the shop, then at Joy, thinking of the question the giant otter had posed. "It's love, I suppose?"

"Obviously," said Joy, with a happy sigh. "Sometimes I wonder, kit, what you would do without me."

Love cures curses.

Fish, Chip, and Ige's voices were louder now. They were clearly coming around the back of the shop to check the annex, and would find Sunlit and Joy at any moment.

"What I'd do without you, Joy?" Sunlit smiled. "Nothing to write home about, that's for sure."

And nothing, she added to herself as their friends came into view, *as curative as this.* For the first time, Sunlit Haven knew for certain that she was in exactly the right place.

Epilogue

Professor Lina McAlpin sat in her office, still wearing scrubs and a name tag, her feet propped up on her desk. Outside her window, dolphins recovering from a short-lived plague frolicked in a large holding tank. But she wasn't to be distracted.

She was alone at the end of another long day. It was difficult running the Marine Center without Sunlit Haven—she'd admit that in a heartbeat.

But she smiled over her latest letter from Seaside.

"Marine Sanctuary," said the professor, her voice confident and practiced in the little room. "I *knew* she'd do well. At last."

Yes—she'd always had complete faith in Haven. As long as the girl could get out of her own way. She was *exactly* the person Seaside had needed.

And this business about the little boy . . . Professor McAlpin tapped Haven's letter against her chin as she stood and rifled through the books stacked on her shelves. With one hand, she managed to extract the one she wanted. *Tales from the Deep: Pelagic Merfolk and Their World.*

An old tome, but one had to take what one could get, when it came to pelagic merfolk. Professor McAlpin had met one only once. Rumors about them abounded; even this supposedly scientific book was more gossip than fact . . .

But she'd always remembered it, because one story in it had

struck her fancy. She found the page immediately.

It is said that pelagic merfolk, like many other sea creatures, do not raise their young themselves. Indeed, very little is known about how these people reproduce. Whether their young are born live or come from eggs, there is much debate; some even theorize that young pelagic merfolk are born out of the sea water, given form by the deepest magic of the ocean itself. Alone, they grow into adulthood and find their path much as fish are drawn back to the waters of their birth to complete their life cycle. No study has been completed, as of yet, on the forces which guide them.

Professor McAlpin traced the excerpt down the page as she read it. Once more she smiled to herself.

She *could* share this information with Sunlit . . . but Lina McAlpin had been in charge of her Marine Center for a very long time. She'd been to a plethora of conferences, read endless papers. She had learned one thing for certain. Some things, the professor felt, do not need to be identified, studied, or taught. They only need to thrive.

About the Author

Elle adores ocean life, magic, and above all, found communities. As a historian and educator, she believes in the value of stories as a mirror for complicated realities. She currently lives in New Jersey with a grumpy tortoise and a three-legged cat.

Find more stories of Sunlit and her friends at ellehart-ford.com. And while you're there, sign up for Elle's newsletter to get bonus material, behind-the-scenes sneak peeks, and terrible jokes!

And if you're curious about Taiwo and Rei's wedding, or Ige's less-than-savory past, check out *Mermaid for Danger* (Alchemical Tales book 3) for the full story!

Also by Elle Hartford

The Alchemical Tales series:
   Beauty and the Alchemist, book 1
   Cold as Snow, book 2
   Mermaid for Danger, book 3
   Cry Big Bad Wolf, book 4
   Cinders to Dust, book 5
   Death Pulls the Strings, book 6
   A Thousand and One Alibis, book 7

Pomegranate Cafe Romance:
   Worthy in Love, book 1
   A Tale of Rowan and Daisy, book 1.5
   Strong in Love, book 2
   Steady in Love, book 3